THE TRICKER-TREATER AND OTHER STORIES

BRIANA MORGAN

To Sam. Thank you for everything.

AUTHOR'S NOTE

The following stories contain graphic violence, blood, gore, religion and religious imagery, body horror, death, gun violence, murder, drowning, possession, mentions of suicide, infidelity, mentions of miscarriage, alcoholism, and implied domestic abuse. Reader discretion is advised.

THE TRICKER-TREATER

MOIRA KICKED SPILLED CANDY CORN OFF HER FRONT STEP. THE remnants of another weeknight massacre, this time all in the name of a holiday.

She'd stopped keeping track of the holidays. They meant nothing, just another day full of shit, another day without Norman in it. What was the point?

She looked at the garden gnome Norman had polished every St. Patrick's Day. The ghost of an old conversation floated back to her as she picked it up from where the kids had knocked it over. Moira closed her eyes and savored the memory.

"It's a gnome, Norm. Not a leprechaun. It's not his holiday."

"I know that! But don't you think what matters is doing it?"

Moira sighed. This St. Patrick's Day she'd grab a rag and polish the years of grime away. So far, she hadn't had the strength. It was the day before Halloween, which meant she'd picked up trash all week, and if those damn kids tried their tricks tonight, she'd give them more than treats.

Movement on the sidewalk, next to the mailbox, caught her eye. Riley stood there, all tousled blond hair and sleepy brown eyes. His hand-me-down sweatshirt needed elbow patches. She'd see to that soon.

"Don't stand there gawking at me. C'mon." She waved him forward, but he looked at his shoes. She put her hands on her hips. "What's the matter with you?"

"He's coming here tonight to get you," he said.

She squinted in the morning sun. "Who's coming to get me?"

"The Tricker-Treater," Riley said. "He's coming here tonight. I made a deal with him."

"What?" Riley never spoke in riddles. He wasn't one to loiter at the end of her driveway either. "Peanut butter cookies inside. Tell me later."

"No, he'll be here later. That's what I'm trying to tell you."

Moira frowned. "Stop listening to your brother. Come inside and have some cookies with me. We'll go from there."

Without waiting to see if he'd follow, Moira headed back into the house. She went straight to the kitchen. The storm door slammed shut not too long after, and Riley pulled up a chair at the kitchen table.

Moira carried the plate of cookies over to him. Up close, he looked like the same old Riley. All she saw was the haunted glint in his eyes, which he got from spending time with his older brother. After school, all he had was Taylor until their mother got home from work. Retail was hell, Moira remembered. When Riley's mother got home, the last thing she'd want to do is scold Taylor for tormenting his little brother.

Norman would have scared Taylor shitless, given the chance. He would have protected Riley. Norman had always been better with kids.

"Lots of trick-or-treaters coming here tomorrow," Moira said. "So what makes yours so special? Why's he coming here tonight?"

Riley froze with his hand halfway to a cookie. "Not trick-or-treater. Tricker-Treater."

Moira shook her head. "I said that."

"No, like . . . hang on." He scooted his chair back from the table and dashed across the room to where the landline rested. There was a small pad of paper beside it, which he snatched up along with a pen before running back to the table. His brow furrowed in concentration. Sticking out his tongue, he leaned over the paper and spelled out the difference for her:

T-R-I-C-K-E-R
T-R-E-A-T-E-R

He set the pen down and waited for her to read his writing. Moira shook her head again. He didn't know how to spell it.

"No 'or,'" he said. "Tricker-Treater. He's both."

Something icy pricked the back of Moira's neck. She brushed her fingers over the spot and found nothing. Her gaze drifted back to the paper.

"He's both?"

"Mm-hm." Riley grabbed a cookie and took a bite. He devoured it, careful not to make eye contact with Moira. It was a sophisticated strategy for a seven-year-old.

Moira leaned on the table and stared at him. "Riley."

He scooted his chair away. "I gotta use the potty."

"Do you or do you not want to talk to me?" she asked.

He stuffed another cookie in his mouth. When he spoke, he sprayed crumbs everywhere. "I don't want to talk about him."

"You mean the Tricker-Treater?"

"Yeah." He choked on the cookie and coughed. Moira grabbed a glass and filled it with water from the sink. She patted him on the back and slid the glass to him.

Riley chugged the water and still couldn't stop coughing. Moira took the plate of cookies from him because no way in hell was he going to choke to death on her watch. Not if she could help it.

3

"You better head on home," Moira said. "You'll worry your mother sick."

Riley scooted back from the table again. "Don't call her. She doesn't know."

"She doesn't know you're here? Did your mom let you stay home from school, or did you play hooky?"

"I . . ." His eyes darted to look over her shoulder. Moira spun around. Nothing there. When she turned back to him, he was heading for the front door.

"Riley!"

"I messed up, I messed up!"

She lunged for his sleeve and missed. He was through the front door and across the yard before she had time to try again. Damn it. What was wrong with that boy? He'd been in no hurry minutes before, when there was a plate of cookies in front of him. The minute she'd mentioned his mother, though . . .

Moira sighed and leaned against the door frame. Something was off with Riley, and she wouldn't let him out of her sight until she understood it.

After a few minutes of eyeing each other across the yard, he returned to the house. Moira stood between him and the front door. "Riley, please. Tell me what's going on."

He chewed his bottom lip. "I don't wanna. I'm scared. It never goes well."

"What do you mean, 'It never goes well'?"

"Every time I tell you, it . . . I messed up," he repeated.

Moira sighed. She was getting nowhere, and fast. Whatever he had on his mind, it upset him so much he wasn't making sense. If she couldn't get him to focus, she would never figure out what was going on. And seeing as how it apparently involved her, she needed to know.

"Riley." Moira grabbed his shoulders and held him there, stooping to look into his eyes. "Whatever you think will happen, I can face it better if you tell me about it, okay?"

His lower lip quivered. "Even if it's bad?"

"Even if it's bad."

Riley gulped. "The Tricker-Treater is gonna stop by your house tonight. You gotta meet with him and do what he says, or else."

Moira quirked an eyebrow at him. "Or else?"

He hesitated. "Like I said, I've told you about him before, and he . . . he always catches you. Even if you run away, he finds you and he . . ." Riley's voice trailed off into a sob. Shiny, fat tears bubbled over his lashes and rolled down his face. Moira pulled him against her and wrapped her arms around him.

Shit, she hadn't meant to make him cry. Jesus Christ, that was the last thing she wanted. Her chest tightened. "It'll be okay, Riley. We'll figure it out together, all right?"

Riley pulled away from her and shook his head. "I dunno."

"I'm older and wiser. Humor me, huh?"

He sniffed and wiped his nose. Moira debated getting a tissue for him, but it was too late—he was already rubbing the snot with his sleeve. As perceptive as the kid could be, he was still a kid, and he was gross.

Sometimes she wondered what it would have been like to have children. Sometimes she watched Riley and was glad that time had passed her.

"You should run home now," Moira said. "Even if you skipped school, your mom won't be angry as long as you're safe."

His gaze jumped over her shoulder again. She waited for him to refocus. He'd come there in such a hurry, and now he kept drifting away. The urgency had waned. That was good.

"Are you feeling all right?"

Riley nodded. "I'm . . . a little better now."

"No more getting upset over the Tricker-Treater, okay?"

Hesitation, then another nod. A slow exhale. "Okay."

5

"You want a few cookies to take home? You can share them with Taylor."

Riley wrinkled his nose at the mention of his brother. "He doesn't deserve cookies."

"I suppose he doesn't."

Moira patted him on the head and went back into the kitchen. She eyed the half-empty water glass in its pool of condensation, the cookie crumbs Riley had sprayed on the table. She looked back at Riley, still standing where she'd left him, and her chest ached. She flattened a hand against her collarbone.

She and Norman could've tried a little longer.

"Riley?"

His head jerked up. "Huh?"

"You still want those cookies?"

"Um . . . no, thanks." He wiped his nose with the sleeve of his sweater again. "I've never stayed this late before. I don't wanna see him."

The poor kid was talking in circles again. Better send him off to someone much more qualified. Moira propped a hand on her hip. "Go on, then. Get outta here before I call your mom. And be careful tomorrow."

Riley cast a long look at her before putting his hand on the doorknob. That was all it took? No fight? No begging her for cookies, saying he changed his mind?

She should have insisted he take some. If he'd still demanded some, that would have been proof things were normal.

Instead, Moira frowned at the back of his head as he walked out and left the door open.

———

MOIRA TOSSED POPCORN INTO HER MOUTH AND WATCHED BILL Murray fail to woo Andie MacDowell. There was no reason for the network to broadcast *Groundhog Day* on October 30, but she wasn't complaining. It had been one of Norman's favorite movies. They'd gone to see it in theaters the day it came out, which seemed so long ago now. Without Norman, time dragged on. How had it only been a year since his death? Watching a movie she'd seen more than a dozen times soothed her ragged nerves. That the movie was itself a perpetual, familiar cycle was not lost on her. In fact, that was a large part of *its* charm—especially tonight, when there was so much on her mind.

Riley's behavior had left her shaken and confused. Sure, he was a kid, but he'd always been perceptive and she trusted what he said. He usually meant what he said. At that age, it was rare for children to have ulterior motives. Whatever Riley thought would happen to her, it was worth considering.

The Tricker-Treater was coming to get her tonight.

Moira's gaze jumped to the glow of the streetlight that permeated her closed blinds. Outside, the air was crisp. Inside, she was cozy.

She drew the knitted afghan tighter around her midsection. Andie slapped Bill. Normally, the moment made Moira laugh. Normally, her nerves weren't wound up like a coiled snake.

The chiming of her doorbell made her jump out of her skin. She jostled the bowl in her lap, spilling popcorn everywhere.

Why was she so jumpy? It was likely Riley and his mother, coming to check on her after their talk. Adriane was nice—she always apologized for Riley with baked goods and wine. When she wasn't working, she tried to come over for tea and to pour out her soul to Moira.

In another life, they could have been mother and daughter. In another life, Norman might still be alive.

Another ache struck Moira's chest. The doorbell chimed again, demanding her attention.

She set the bowl aside and stood. Whoever it was, they were

insistent. She doubted they'd go away if she ignored them. Probably some damn kids, anyway. God willing, they wouldn't egg her when she opened the door—for their sakes and hers. She didn't feel forgiving.

Moira crept to the door and pulled back the curtain on the window beside it. There was no one there.

Puzzled, she let the curtain drop and stood on tiptoe to look through the peephole.

No one.

Moira stepped back. She flattened a hand against her chest. The doorbell chimed again.

Icy dread stuck its fingers down the back of Moira's shirt. Her hand settled on the cold metal doorknob. After a breath, she twisted it and pulled the front door open.

She gasped.

The man—if anyone could even call the thing a man—stood at least seven or eight feet tall. It had to double over to fit under the awning of her porch. Pale red skin stretched tight over pointed features, most notably a bear skull. At least, she thought it was a bear skull. Norman would have known for sure. Norman always knew.

Coal-black eyes glittered at her as the thing bared its teeth—razor-sharp—in a smile. It wore nothing but a top hat, which it tipped before it spoke.

"I hope you were expecting me."

His voice was low and smooth, like a jazz singer's, and she shivered. Moira supposed she should have fainted or had a heart attack by then, but once he spoke, all her fear disappeared. It was like he had swallowed it up with his words.

"Who are you?" she asked.

"Riley didn't tell you? I'm the Tricker-Treater. Would you mind if I came in?"

Moira froze with her hand still on the doorknob. What was she supposed to do? The Tricker-Treater offered the illusion of a choice. Was it merely that—an illusion—or would he let her decide how the evening would progress? Moira let her gaze wander over the creature's form again. He had the emaciated look of a feral dog, and the tightness in her chest only tightened even further. Nothing about him made her think he'd give her any choice.

"C-come in," Moira said.

The Tricker-Treater kept his eyes locked on her as he stepped over the threshold and into the house. Moira swore he brought the smell of decay inside with him, but a moment later, it vanished.

Rotting pumpkins, she thought. That was the smell.

Moira gestured for him to sit on the couch. Eldritch horror or not, he was a guest.

The Tricker-Treater sat, bones creaking and popping as he did so. Moira tried her damnedest not to wince at the noises. She sat in Norman's favorite armchair and waited for the Tricker-Treater to speak.

"Has Riley told you all about me?" he asked.

Moira paused. "How do you know Riley?"

"We made a deal. He's a special child, isn't he? Perceptive. Tenacious." The Tricker-Treater flashed her another chilling smile. "Fragile."

The blood dropped from Moira's face. "What are you getting at?"

The Tricker-Treater steepled his long, bony fingers. "It would be a shame if any danger were to befall Riley. If you could prevent such a tragedy, wouldn't you want to, no matter the cost?"

Moira rubbed the goosebumps on her arms. "Don't you dare hurt him."

"We made a deal," the Tricker-Treater repeated. "He asked for money so his mother could be around more often. I told him I could give him anything he wanted—such as money—for a price."

The Tricker-Treater's eyes made Moira's head swim. She broke eye contact. "So that's why you're here. To kill me."

She should have known this would be how she died. Norman, with all his superstitions and wonder of the paranormal, had died of a stroke in the kitchen. A nice, normal death. Meanwhile, here she was, about to be whisked away by a monster for the sake of a child's wish.

"Not quite," the Tricker-Treater said. "Well, only if I must."

Moira's head snapped up and she met his gaze again, even though it dizzied her. "What's that supposed to mean?"

The Tricker-Treater tapped his claws against the coffee table. *Click, click, click.* "If you play by the rules, everything will be all right."

The sinking feeling in Moira's gut returned. "What rules?"

The Tricker-Treater's unnerving smile also returned. "Every game has rules, Moira. Do you want to play?"

Her stomach had dropped to her ass, and she didn't think it would resurface anytime soon. Whoever this man—or creature —was, he wasn't going anywhere until he got what he wanted from her.

"What happens if I don't want to play the game?" she asked.

"You lose."

"And what happens if I lose?"

"Then Taylor wins." The Tricker-Treater's smile tore across his face. "And I take you away forever."

Moira's throat constricted. So he wanted to kill her. Even if he acted like she had a choice, she didn't. Riley had already chosen for her. He had sealed her fate.

But what did Taylor have to do with it?

"Taylor?" she asked.

"To fulfill Riley's deal, I must receive a sacrifice. He had to present me with someone he loves and someone he hates to play the game. I balance the scales. The loser dies."

Jesus Christ. What had Riley done?

"He's too young to make a deal like that," she said. "You're taking advantage of him."

"I don't discriminate," he said. "A wish is a wish, and I must grant it. You must play the game, or you will die. These are my conditions."

"What if Taylor and I both refuse? You only need to kill one of us, right? And you seem reasonable. You wouldn't kill us to prove a point."

"No." The Tricker-Treater's smile twisted into something darker, more feral. Moira wanted to scream, but panic kept her gaze fixed on his face. "With two refusals, I take the wish-maker instead."

Moira gulped. "You'd kill Riley?"

"*Kill* is such a boring word for what I do, but yes. Riley would become the sacrifice." He steepled his fingers again. "But you always have a choice."

Did he think she'd let Riley die? She must have been Riley's "someone he loves," which meant the Tricker-Treater had to know she loved him too. She couldn't damn him.

"I'll play," Moira said.

"Wonderful. Let's go."

The Tricker-Treater snapped his fingers, Moira felt a tug, and the world went dark.

———

THE REEK OF IRON PULLED MOIRA FROM UNCONSCIOUSNESS. HER eyelids snapped open, pupils unfocused as they sought the light. Only a spare bulb hung overhead, struggling through the shadows. A familiar teenage form swam into view, fastened to a chair by ropes.

Taylor.

A shadow skulked off to Taylor's left, and Moira's gaze

floated over to it. A long, lanky figure broke from the blackness and formed a solid shape. Sharp teeth glittered in the light as the creature grinned.

The Tricker-Treater.

He snapped his fingers again, and the lightbulb shattered. Moira went to shield her face from the exploding glass, but ropes restrained her. The Tricker-Treater had tied her down too.

A brilliant light enveloped the room, blinding Moira for a minute. The light faded to a ball that hovered over the Tricker-Treater's head. It was small, but somehow bright enough for her to make out everything in the room, including Taylor.

She looked back at the boy. Blood dripped from ragged scratches in his cheek and stained the front of his shirt. That must have been the source of the iron smell.

Moira looked to the Tricker-Treater for an explanation.

"He struggled," he said, "so I had to be rough. But he's learned his lesson. Haven't you, Taylor?"

Taylor groaned and twisted against the ropes. The Tricker-Treater clicked his tongue and wagged a finger at Taylor. He froze.

"Think it's time for me to explain the rules of the game to you both," the Tricker-Treater said. "But no cheating. Is that understood?"

Moira still didn't know what was going on, but she nodded. Whatever game he had in mind, she had to win, for Riley's sake. She didn't know what would happen to Taylor, except that he might die. She'd cross that bridge when she came to it.

Across the room, Taylor grunted.

The Tricker-Treater gave a wet, hacking cough. Moira watched it rattle his prominent ribcage. Had he not been so frightening, she might have worried for him. As it was, she wished the cough had been worse.

The Tricker-Treater pulled another chair away from the

table. It scraped across the floor with a sound that bit Moira's eardrums. She flinched. He lowered his long body into the chair and removed his hat, exposing his shiny, red baldness.

"I will now explain the rules, and I will not repeat myself. You both must pay attention if you want to win."

"I don't give a shit about winning," Taylor said. "I don't even want to play. I don't give a shit about Riley."

A muscle jerked in Moira's jaw. What an asshole. Did this kid understand what he was saying?

"That's not what you told me earlier," the Tricker-Treater said. "You agreed to play the game because you wanted him to live."

Moira almost didn't believe it, but the Tricker-Treater had no motive to lie. He stretched a hand toward Taylor, and Taylor's eyes widened. The Tricker-Treater's razor-like claws glittered in the light.

"You'll play," he said, "or Riley dies."

Taylor shut his eyes. "Okay, okay, but please don't hurt me."

"It isn't me you should worry about."

Moira swallowed a curse. As much as she hated to cooperate with this *thing*, it seemed they had no choice. If she didn't play the Tricker-Treater's game, Riley would die. She wouldn't let that happen.

"What do I have to do?" she asked.

The Tricker-Treater's smile widened. Moira withheld a shiver. Taylor flattened himself against the back of the chair, trying to get as far away as possible.

"Once I untie you both," the Tricker-Treater said, putting his hat back on, "you'll have fifteen minutes to choose a weapon and determine the sacrifice."

Moira frowned. "Kill each other?"

"So *vulgar*," he replied.

"I don't want to kill an old lady," Taylor said.

Like he even could if he wanted to, Moira thought. In her own

13

way, she agreed—she didn't want to kill him, and she didn't want to die. But Riley couldn't die either. She'd do what she could, whatever she *had* to. It wasn't a choice.

"Where are the weapons?" Moira asked.

Taylor gaped at her. "We don't have to do this!"

"I detest idle chatter," the Tricker-Treater said. "Such a waste of precious time."

Moira stiffened at his words. Did that mean they'd started? Were they supposed to get going? Why was she still tied up, then? The Tricker-Treater had said—

A click of his fingers and her bindings dissolved. Fuck, she had to get moving. She liked the word *fuck*, although Norman never had. The way his face used to scrunch up when she said it to him—

"Moira," the Tricker-Treater warned. "You don't have time for reminiscing."

She chose not to dwell on the discomfort of having him inside her mind in favor of finding a weapon. But where the fuck were they?

Taylor was squealing something she didn't care to listen to. She didn't want to kill him, but they would soon be out of time, and if she did nothing—whether or not he killed her—Riley was in danger.

Moira dragged herself out of the chair and looked around the room. It was still difficult to see, with the only lighting coming from the ball conjured by the Tricker-Treater, but they were surrounded by boxes of all shapes and sizes.

Taylor leaped up from his chair and dove headfirst into the box behind him, digging like a dumpster-diver in search of castoff treasures. Shit, she had to get a move on or he'd kill her with whatever he found.

Moira started with a box on her left, plain cardboard on the outside, unassuming enough. As she dug through a pile of moth-eaten clothes, a sharp edge bit into her palm. She cried out. Upon further, much more hesitant inspection, she discovered the source of the wound—a Japanese samurai sword.

That's a katana, Norm corrected in her head.

Moira didn't have time to smile. She wrapped her fingers around the base of the sword and pulled just as Taylor came sprinting toward her with a hatchet in his hands. The metal glinted as he brought it down, right as Moira darted out of the way.

"Jesus, Taylor!"

"Stand *still!*"

He lifted the hatchet and swung it down again, with Moira only narrowly dodging it this time. She was close enough to hear the *whoosh* of the blade as it came down past her face. As she ducked to the side, so did Taylor. His third hit struck her shoulder. White-hot flames lit Moira's muscles and leaked pain down her arm. Warm blood dripped off her elbow.

Jesus *fuck,* that hurt.

Movement caught the corner of her eye and she whirled around, still clutching her injured shoulder. Taylor raised the hatchet again. She had to get out of his way.

Still carrying the sword, Moira feinted left. Taylor took the bait and swung. She moved right, raised the sword, hesitated—

The light went out. Moira couldn't see one inch in front of her face. Distantly, the Tricker-Treater's claws clicked against a hard surface. *Dragged* against it, more like.

Moira shivered.

Mooooiiiiraaaaaaaaa . . .

She jabbed with the sword, wincing as the blade bounced off the wall. It almost relieved her that she hadn't hit Taylor.

Something rough brushed her calf. She jerked back, swallowing a cry. Something metal clattered to the ground, and Taylor yelped.

"Don't move, Taylor."

"Are w-we out of time?" As brave and seemingly blood-

15

thirsty as he'd been moments before, his voice shook. Hatchet or not, he was only a kid. He had his entire life ahead of him.

And she'd tried to kill him.

Moira let go of the katana. It, too, clattered to the floor. "What's up with turning the lights off, huh? Not fucked up enough as it is?"

"I assumed it would be easier for you to kill him with the lights off," the Tricker-Treater said. "That way, you wouldn't have to see him."

"Whose side are you on?" Taylor countered. His voice had an edge to it that scared her, sharpened by fear into a pointed rage. It made him sound dangerous.

She didn't think he had the strength to kill her, but fear could drive someone to do the unthinkable. And she'd let go of her weapon.

"I believe in leveling the playing field," the Tricker-Treater said. "Moira is, shall we say, more *experienced* in life, and Taylor has more energy. We correct this discrepancy with darkness."

Moira swallowed. In theory, everything he said made sense. But all she could think about was that there must be something she'd overlooked, something the Tricker-Treater had overlooked. A loophole.

Some way to save Riley without having to kill his brother.

She had to pick up the katana again. Without it, she was powerless. There was still a chance Taylor would rediscover his bravado, would run toward her again with the hatchet raised, would bring it down and—

The Tricker-Treater chuckled in the gloom, and Moira knew he'd been inside her head again. Shit, that was . . . inconvenient. How could she try to find a loophole if he listened in on everything she thought?

Get the fuck out of my head.

Again, the Tricker-Treater chuckled. "Manners, Moira. But I

would be remiss not to heed your request, as vulgar as you might have phrased it. All you had to do was ask."

Moira gaped at him in the darkness—or, at least, she gaped in what she assumed was his direction. It was still impossible to see anything, and though the Tricker-Treater had claimed he was just leveling the playing field, Moira couldn't understand how this could help her.

Distantly, Taylor whimpered. Could he be afraid of the dark?

"Please," he said. "Turn on the lights."

The Tricker-Treater's claws clicked together as he contemplated Taylor's request. "Moira, what do you think?"

What did she think? This whole twisted game was a goddamn mess. It was ludicrous that this demon expected her to kill a child, or the child to kill her. She would do almost anything to save Riley because she loved him, but she wasn't sure she could do this.

Most of all, Moira thought she had already lost. She had to change her mind somehow, or else she really would. *Find the loophole*, she reminded herself. There had to be an angle she hadn't yet considered.

Moira shuffled her feet. The point of the katana bit into her shin and she fought the urge to cry out. Warm liquid seeped from the wound—not too much, but not too little to escape her notice. The darkness heightened everything. Tentatively, she bent over and fumbled around for the handle, praying her fingers wouldn't graze the blade. At last, they closed around fabric—the binding on the handle—and she pulled it up with both hands as she rose to a standing position.

"Moira," the Tricker-Treater prompted again. And the idea came to her. If she could kill the Tricker-Treater, she could end the game. She'd win without killing Taylor, and Riley would be safe.

She knew next to nothing about the Tricker-Treater's fortitude, although he seemed like a formidable foe. She had to give it a shot. Anything was better than plunging the blade into Taylor.

"Turn on the lights," Moira answered.

She tightened her grip on the blade and widened her stance to give her more stability. Sweat trickled down the side of her neck. Her heart beat so loudly it threatened to deafen her, but she stayed grounded. She didn't have a choice.

The Tricker-Treater snapped his fingers and the lights flickered on again. Moira coordinated her attack with the fluorescent flash. She ran full speed, katana thrust forward like a jousting lance. Taylor gasped, eyes widening in horror—until Moira jabbed the sword into the Tricker-Treater's gut.

"Shit!" Taylor yelled.

The Tricker-Treater didn't flinch. He didn't scream, nor did he indicate that she had hit him. Instead, he wrapped his clawed fingers around the blade and looked right at Moira. The twisted grin he produced was the worst thing she'd ever seen.

"Well, now. Isn't this *exciting?*"

Moira trembled, but she didn't let go of the handle. If she did, she was afraid he'd turn the blade on her. Taylor crept closer to the scene, face ashen. He was trembling, too, even as he reached out to take the sword from Moira.

She shook her head vehemently. "You're not responsible for this. Taylor, if anything happens—"

"It isn't polite to speak about others as though they aren't there," the Tricker-Treater chimed in. He was still holding the blade, still the picture of tranquility even with the sword sticking out of his stomach and his black blood dripping from the wound onto the floor. "I wonder if you two have forgotten your manners."

"Fuck you," Taylor spat.

Moira had to agree, though she couldn't find the words. All she could focus on was the blood, the way it poured from the

Tricker-Treater's stomach even though the wound was technically still sealed up.

The Tricker-Treater flexed his claws, and his grin widened. The blade slipped out of Moira's hands.

"Taylor!" Moira shouted.

The blade shot backward out of the Tricker-Treater's stomach and whirled around to point at Taylor. He reacted a second too late. Moira stared in horror as the black, blood-stained tip pushed into Taylor's chest. He stiffened, limbs flying out, mouth open, eyes the size of galaxies—

Then his body dropped. It made a sick *thwack* as it landed.

Moira turned her head and puked. When she turned back, the Tricker-Treater hunched over, holding his hat in his hands. He had the decency not to grin.

"Oh, dear," he said. "This is less than ideal."

If she weren't so afraid, she would have smacked him. "'Less than ideal'? A child is dead! You fucking *killed* him, you son of a bitch."

"If I hadn't, you would have."

"I wouldn't have," she insisted. "You've been inside my head. You must have known I wouldn't."

"Hmph." The Tricker-Treater twisted his hat in his hands. He was having trouble looking Moira in the eye. "Well, this presents a challenge."

She wrangled the urge to strangle him. "What are you talking about?"

"The rules of the game were clear. To save Riley, there must be a sacrifice." He paused, as though waiting for her to remember the rules. "One of you must kill the other."

"But we can't now. Taylor's dead." Realization dawned on Moira, eclipsing the fear. "*You* killed him. That's the loophole."

"So it would seem." If Moira's search for a loophole upset him, it didn't show. He was so lost in contemplation he paid her

19

no mind. She could have attacked him then. Taylor's hatchet lay on the floor close to his body. If she leaned forward a little—

"Unfortunately," he said. "Riley must perish."

All the blood drained from Moira's face. *Like hell he must.* "What are you talking about? I played your stupid game. Taylor . . . well, that means I won. Those were your rules, remember?"

"Alas, Moira, that isn't the case." The Tricker-Treater clicked his tongue. "Neither of you did as I asked, as I *required* of you, so there is no winner. And, as there's no winner, you forfeit Riley's life. I'm afraid *those* are the rules."

Moira's stomach roiled. There had to be another way. She had to save Riley somehow, or Taylor had died for nothing. She refused to lose Riley, refused to let his mother bury *both* her sons.

"Take me instead," she pleaded.

The Tricker-Treater hesitated. "That wasn't part of the deal. You only forfeit your life if the other participant takes it. As the other participant is dead, there is no reason for your life to end."

His logic and politeness made her want to tear her hair out. "Taylor shouldn't have died. I didn't kill him. Doesn't that change up your shitty rules somehow?"

Again, he hesitated. His face twisted up as though he were in pain. "I concede that Taylor's departure was unnecessary, given the game's aim. Reckless, even. However, there must be some punishment for you." The Tricker-Treater looked pointedly at the hole in his gut. "You also broke the rules."

"You never said I couldn't attack you," she argued.

His mouth twitched. "Fair enough. Hm . . . what do you think I should do to you, Moira? What sort of fate would be fair?"

Moira's tongue sat like lead in her mouth. How was she supposed to make such a strange decision? The question wasn't one she'd planned for. He wasn't in her head anymore, so she wondered if she could just throw something out there, something far from "fair," in terms of extremity. Or perhaps he already knew what he would do to her, and he was just playing another sick game?

"Tick-tock," the Tricker-Treater said.

Moira swallowed. Hard. If Norm were here, he'd have the perfect idea. He was always so wise, her Norm, even when he was being silly. The last time they'd watched *Groundhog Day* together, he'd said—

Groundhog Day. Yes, that was the answer. It was the only way for her to atone while still paying homage to her husband. It was the only way to make sure Riley's mother got her son back —and got to keep Riley too.

Moira didn't look forward to that fate, but she accepted it.

She gave the Tricker-Treater a watery smile. "Have you seen any Bill Murray movies?"

———

WHEN MOIRA CAME TO, SWEAT DRENCHED HER CLOTHING. Sunlight streamed through the blinds, and birds chirped outside. *Jesus.* She felt like a train had run her over.

Out of habit, even after a year, she rolled over to look at Norm's side of the bed. She smoothed a hand over the blankets and sighed. "Miss you more than ever, hon."

Outside, the distant hum of a mower pierced the air. She must have slept in much later than usual. A glance at the clock on her nightstand confirmed her suspicions, and she groaned. That would teach her to go through a bottle of wine by herself.

Pain flared in Moira's shoulder. When she reached for it, the feeling vanished. She checked under her shirt. Nothing.

Must just be part of getting old.

It seemed like a nice day, what with the birds chirping and the sunlight and all. Maybe she'd crawl out of bed and do something fun for a change, bake some cookies to give to the neighbor's kid, Riley. Maybe he'd share with his overworked mother. Poor Adriane worked more than she was home, and Moira recognized her exhaustion.

An hour later saw her dressed and pulling fresh cookies from the oven, the smell filling the house like a bug bomb—albeit a delicious one. While she waited for the cookies to cool, she slipped on her shoes and went outside to fetch the paper.

Moira kicked spilled candy corn off her front step. The remnants of another weeknight massacre, this time all in the name of a holiday.

She'd stopped keeping track of the holidays.

MORATORIUM

THE PICTURE RESTS WHERE IT'S BEEN SINCE THE DAY MY MOTHER died. Aside from the photo, the kitchen table is bare. We never eat at the table—it's become a shrine—but I revisit the table and the picture every night.

My father never looks at this picture anymore.

In it, my parents' backs are turned to the camera as they gaze out at the sunset over the rolling hills. My mother is the picture of health on the day she was married. Her full shoulders are plump with a vitality I haven't seen since I was a little girl. Her dark hair is short. She's not wearing her wedding veil because it annoyed her. My father told me she hated that veil.

In the photo, he tilts his head to rest against my mother's. He's been gray now for so long that I almost don't recognize the young man in the picture. His hair is the color of freshly stained wood, untouched by the passage of time. His shoulders are relaxed, not hunched as they are nowadays. His back is straight. Even though I can't see his face, I'm certain he's smiling.

My mother didn't smile.

She leans against my father with her bare head pressing into his shoulder. Her right arm is linked through his as though she never wants to let him go. His grip on her is bruising.

In an hour I will move the picture to the counter so I can dust the table, per my father's mandate. I will forget to put it back when I have finished, and I will pay for my mistake tomorrow. Later, when I go to bed, my father will creep down into the kitchen. He will open the refrigerator in order to see better. His fingers will find the photo in its temporary location and he will caress its surface without looking at it before transferring it back to the table. He will pour himself a glass of milk. He will close the fridge. He will go back to bed.

In the photo, I wonder if his tie is loose. He hated that damn tie, but not as much as my mother must have when he wrapped it around her throat.

THE DIVE

CLIVE MITCHELL SWIMS TOWARD THE SURFACE OF THE WATER without knowing what's in store. With every kick he soars higher and higher, until his head breaks the surface and he gasps for air. The boat floats only a meter away from him, yet it's all he can do not to burst as he swims toward it. His lungs sting and his throat burns like hellfire, but it's over. The horror is at last finished, now behind him.

His fingers brush the boat's hull and strong arms drag him out of the water and onto the deck, where he flops like a fish. The wetsuit and gravity put a strain on his already worn-out body. He wants to sleep forever. More than anything, he wants to cry. He looks up at Harry and shakes his head. "One hell of a dive, man."

Harry bites his lip. "But did you find it?"

"Yeah, of course."

Clive beams at him and kneels to remove the object from the pocket of the wetsuit: a small black velvet box.

"What do you think, Harry?"

"Is it even in there?"

"Of course it's bloody in there, why else would I have come up?"

"Fine," Harry says. "It's all just so *fine*." He cradles the box to his chest like it's the infant he lost the year before. "And you're sure this is hers, before we take it any further."

The words come out as more of a statement than a question, but Clive nods. "It has to be. You think someone else would have dropped that in the ocean?"

Harry shrugs. "Could have, yeah."

"No way."

"Well, it's possible."

Clive feels sick to his stomach. He snatches the box from his brother's hands. Its weight is soothing. "You're not the only one who lost something that day."

Harry's eyes darken. "You're kidding me."

Clive all but growls. "My girlfriend, Harry. Remember my girlfriend?"

"Your bloody *girlfriend*. Meanwhile, I lost my son and the mother of my child."

Clive shakes his head. He reaches up behind his shoulders and pulls down the wetsuit's zipper. It comes down with a satisfying *prrrip*. Then, he peels the wet rubber from his skin and basks in the freedom that the open air provides him. His flesh cools.

Harry sighs, and his chest moves in and out. The breath rattles in his throat. "I'm sorry," he says. "That was a low blow. I shouldn't have—"

"No," Clive says. "Don't say it."

The boat bobs softly in the water and waves lap against the hull.

Harry scratches the scar on the side of his nose. "We both have baggage, let's leave it at that. But we also have each other."

Clive nods and plays with the silver chain around his neck. "I didn't even think I'd find it. I was halfway to the bottom when I started to despair. It's so murky down there, Harry, you can't see a bloody thing. When my fins touched the ground, I still couldn't find it. I scraped along in the sand for ten minutes."

"I know," Harry says.

"And then I turned around, and it was wedged up in the coral. Just sitting there, lit up by a patch of sunlight, as though it was waiting for me." Clive looks out at the ocean, but he hears the squealing of brakes and the crunch of metal, of glass and bone—

"Harry," he says. "Harry . . . did you go and see it?"

Harry's Adam's apple bobs. He doesn't talk for a minute. "I had to."

"You would," Clive says.

"I had to see it. Damn it if I couldn't stop myself from going there." The next thing that happens, Harry is crying. Tears stream down his cheeks and his hands curl into fists. Rage consumes him. "And I hate myself for what I said that day. I hate myself sometimes."

"I can't stop thinking about it," Clive says. "If you hadn't divorced Georgia, if I hadn't started dating her, if I'd just called them a bloody cab—"

"It isn't your fault. You know it isn't."

"Nor yours."

Clive slips his fingers into the lip at the front of the little box. "Want me to go ahead and open this thing?"

Harry walks to the port side of the boat and leans on the railing. "Do you want to open it?"

"That isn't necessary."

"All right, then. Open it."

An uncomfortable silence swallows the boat, as though the ocean and the seagulls are no longer in existence. The discarded wetsuit squishes as Clive kneels down on it. He doesn't trust himself to stand. Next, he uses his nails to pry open the box, and he peers anxiously inside. He says nothing.

"What's the matter?"

"Harry," Clive says, "it isn't in here."

"What do you mean?"

"The necklace is missing."

Harry staggers backward as though he's been shot. The wetsuit squishes as he stumbles over it. In an instant, he's standing in front of Clive looking angrier than Clive has ever seen him. "Where'd you put it?" he asks.

"What do you mean, where'd I put it?"

"The necklace. Where is it?"

Suddenly, Clive knows he's in trouble. His hands tremble as he sets the box on the captain's seat. "Take a deep breath. How was I supposed to know the necklace wouldn't be in there?"

"You're the one who brought it up. You're the one who touched it."

"I didn't bloody take it out if that's what you're implying."

"I'm not implying, I'm outright stating."

"I didn't touch the bloody necklace."

"It sure as hell didn't swim."

Clive scratches his head. "I didn't take it. Either someone found it first, we've got the wrong box, or there was never any necklace to begin with."

"It was there," Harry says. "You can't say it wasn't there." He paces the deck of the boat, shoving his hands into his pockets. "The note said it would be here. The note gave us the coordinates. There's no other explanation. Someone must've taken it."

"I have no idea what could've happened."

In an instant, Harry is in Clive's face, gripping his forearms hard enough to bruise. As he speaks, Clive smells the beer on his breath. "You *told* me it was in there."

"I didn't take the necklace!"

Harry hauls off and punches Clive square in the nose. There's a loud crack, and blood streams down Clive's face. His eyes water. "What the hell are you doing?"

Harry's face purples. "Where the hell is—"

"I don't *know!*" Clive says. "I told you, I have no idea. And you didn't have to punch me in the bloody face, for God's sakes." He claps a hand over his nose and winces at the knife of pain that stabs him between his eyes. "Ow. Damn it."

Slowly, Harry's face transitions from purple to red, from red to white. "Is it broken?"

"Feels like it."

Harry sits behind the wheel with his face in his hands. Clive probes his nose, winces, and sits on a padded bench. Waves lap against the hull and rock the craft from side to side. Above, the overcast sky promises rain. Coming out this far with a storm approaching was risky, but they believed it was worth the risk. Now, Clive isn't sure they made the right choice.

Thunder rumbles in the distance. Harry curses.

"We should head back," Clive says. "Try to beat the rain."

"We already can't beat it."

"No, but maybe we can dock before the worst of it sets in."

Harry drops his hands from his face. "I'm not giving up until we've found the necklace."

Clive winces again. "It's gone, mate. We've been over this. The box was shut tight, there's no way—"

"The *note*," Harry says. "The note . . . it said, it told us—"

"It didn't mention the necklace."

Clive wipes blood from his mouth. Most of it has dried and sticks to the skin above his upper lip. He'll need warm water to get it off. Soap and warm water. They're so far from land now, maybe it will be hours before he gets the chance to wash the blood off his face. Maybe the rain will wash it off for him.

The rain. A few fat droplets spatter on Clive's thigh. Harry lifts his head to the sky. His frown deepens.

"We should go now," Clive says.

But Harry keeps quiet, now staring at his hands. The wheels

turn in his head, and Clive knows what he'll say next because he knows his older brother better than he knows himself.

"It was supposed to be here. The note said, 'buried treasure.'"

"'Buried treasure, heart's desire,'" Clive quotes.

Like Harry, he read the note so many times he memorized it. All the sloping lines in Georgia's neat handwriting . . . he'd felt her in the ink, in the movements of the pen on the paper. For a minute, it was enough to make him forget she wasn't coming back. It was enough to make him forget Jasper, and to some extent, Harry.

Now it all comes flooding back.

If you want her so bad, mate, fucking take her. But you have to take him too.

You don't know he's mine, Harry.

You don't know he isn't.

Clive looks over at Harry again. Harry meets Clive's eyes and clenches his jaw like he knows what Clive is thinking. Clive flashes back to their childhood, sitting on the driveway playing Lego as the sun beat down on them. Throwing his arms around Harry's neck, hugging him until Harry made him let go. Writing "my brother" as the answer to the question, "Who's your favorite person?"

How far they have come.

Lightning rips through the inky clouds above them. Fatter raindrops fall now, wet the back of Clive's neck and pool in his hair. Saltwater stings his eyes and he doesn't know whether it's ocean or tears. Maybe it's both.

"Do you have it?" Clive's voice struggles to overcome the thunder and the downpour that breaks out.

Harry nods. His hand dips into the pocket of his shirt and emerges with the too-familiar slip of paper, folded into fourths. As though unwrapping an offering, he takes his time unfolding it and smoothing out the creases. Harry hunches over to shield the paper with his body.

Clive scoots to the other end of the padded bench and holds a hand out to Harry. "May I?"

Harry puts the paper in his hand. He hesitates. "Out loud, please."

"Of course." Clive studies the note. Georgia's handwriting almost undoes him then, more so than it did the first time he looked at it. He isn't sure why. Something about seeing it in these strange circumstances shakes him to his core. Like Harry, he hunches forward to protect the note from the rain. He clears his throat and raises his voice to be heard above the din.

"'My boys, my bravest men. If you're reading this, something terrible has happened to me. I'm young and fairly healthy and have no reason to think the worst could happen. You know I always think it's better to be safe than sorry. I haven't any formal will, and maybe that's what I should be writing instead of this, but I fear the lawyers can't grasp my relationships with you. We are all entangled and we're oh-so-complicated. I want to leave you both my most prized possession. After my death, I want you to discover my buried treasure. My heart's desire. The coordinates are below. Love you madly, Georgia.'"

Clive basks in the words and the memory of her voice. Harry lets out a shuddering sigh. The rain comes down in sheets now, lightning rending the sky, thunder crashing around them. It's only a matter of time before the waves get out of hand and overtake them. The water rocks the boat. If only they'd thought to wear life vests. Clive can swim well enough in calm water, but Harry can't swim at all.

"Mum's necklace," Harry murmurs. "Has to be."

"'Most prized possession,'" Clive repeats. "You gave it to her and she still wore it with me. Knew how much it meant to us."

He pictures it now, a teardrop ruby pendant on a gold chain, and his stomach drops. If he shuts his eyes, he remembers it dangling from their mother's neck as she leaned over them to serve them peas at dinner. He recalls how it glinted in the sunlight, reflecting up into his mother's eyes. He remembers his mother giving the necklace to Harry, telling him it would be perfect for welcoming his new bride into the family.

And, as hard as he tries not to, Clint sees himself at his mother's grave, one arm around Harry and the other around Georgia, all of them crying impossibly hard.

Georgia had been so thrilled to see the two of them together, even then. Even though she and Harry had already broken up and she'd started dating Clint.

It was never about the necklace.

"Heart's desire," he murmurs.

Harry shields his eyes from the downpour that nonetheless drips down his face. "What are you talking about?"

"Don't think the necklace was ever in there, Harry. Wasn't she buried with it?"

"I . . ." Harry considers his words for a moment, frowning. "Closed casket. I don't—"

But Clive remembers. He can't help recalling Jasper's small, damp hand in his. The cloying scent of too much perfume and cologne as his loved ones leaned in to hug him. The glossy, dark surface of the casket as it lay beneath the incandescent lights. Clive remembers because he can never forget, and that's his curse.

"She was," Clive finishes. "I had to bring it to the funeral home. Jasper helped me find it. *Jesus*, we are thick."

Harry shakes his head. "I still don't get it."

"Her heart's desire wasn't the necklace. She wanted us to be together."

"No," Harry says. "But you—the box, right? What was the box doing there if not for the necklace?"

"Bloody coincidence. I don't know."

"Exactly where she said it would be?"

"I don't fucking *know*." Clive drags a hand down his face.

"I don't believe in coincidence."

"You don't believe in anything. I had to drag your ass out here with me, on this boat, and now it's fucking storming and you don't want to go back."

"It's too late to go back."

"You think I don't know that?" A muscle jerks in Clive's jaw. He's being unreasonable, but it's an unreasonable time. And Harry needs to hear it. Clive needs to get it all out while he can. "I'm not as stupid as you think I am."

Harry balks. "I never said you were stupid."

"You didn't have to. All those years, when we were younger . . . the looks, the snide remarks . . . you think I didn't see or hear any of that? And what you told Georgia, told *Jasper*, even. They shared all that with me."

"I . . . I didn't think . . ." Harry's voice trails off.

"No, but you should have." Clive is yelling now, not only to be heard above the awful weather, but to get his point across. If Harry misses this, Clive will not get another chance. He has to lay it all out for his brother. "All Georgia ever wanted was for us to get along. Maybe we're not supposed to, though. Maybe we've never really gotten along."

"We played together all the time as kids, Clive. We loved each other."

"We did, yeah. As much as we could," Clive relents. Tears prick his eyes, and as he speaks again, his voice catches. "I still bloody love you, Harry, but there's been too much between us. We've made a right mess of things."

"We can clean it up."

"We can't. Don't you understand? This was an effort, yeah?" Clive sobs, hiccups as he pushes past his tears to talk. "One thing we had to do, and we can't fucking do it right. We're going to die out here."

"You don't know that."

"Neither do you."

The men fall silent. The only sounds for miles are peals of

33

thunder and heavy rain hitting the water. Clive gets up from the padded bench and paces the length of the boat. It's a dinghy in the best of circumstances and it's far too small to make it through a storm of this size. Already, water pools in puddles on the deck. Clive kicks off his shoes so he doesn't slip. The deck is cool beneath his feet and somewhat reassuring. It reminds him this is real, it's happening, he's here.

"I love you too," Harry says.

Clive's throat tightens. There is so much he wants to say, but the words will never come. More lightning, more thunder, more rain. None of it matters anymore.

Harry gets up from behind the wheel. His shoes make him slide, but he catches himself. His dark hair is disheveled, and his eyes are tired. The boat bobs like a cork and jostles both men. They stumble. Clive catches Harry by the arms and they stand there for a minute, holding each other, holding their gazes.

How can Harry's eyes, the same blue as Clive's, look so foreign to him now? So *frightened*.

Harry cries, too, and no more words are needed.

The ocean swells up and simmers around them. Rising waves reflect the flashing lightning.

They are going to die out here.

"I'm sorry," Clive says.

"I am too. For everything."

Clive pulls his brother in for a hug and Harry holds on to him for dear life. The two of them are still locked in an embrace when a wave lifts the boat and sends it surging forward for another wave to overtake it. The water flips the boat and the two men plunge into the ocean.

The darkness and the warmth beneath the waves are overwhelming. How can it be so hot down here?

Saltwater stings Clive's eyes, fills his mouth. It coats the inside of his lungs. He kicks and thrashes and keeps his eyes open in hopes he'll see Harry. Another flash of lightning illuminates the water, and he can barely make out his brother's flailing shape, arms and legs akimbo as he also struggles to move.

Air bubbles swirl around Clive in the water, coil around his torso. His body spasms. His throat seizes and his jaw drops open, gasping and pulling at water. How long have they been under?

Harry's closer to him now. His eyes bulge, and Clive fears that his look the same. Harry's arms shoot out as if reaching for Clive, but they can't help each other. There's no help for them down here.

The saltwater chokes Clive, makes him cough so hard he gags, but he can't catch his breath. Not here. Maybe hell is real, and they've found it in the ocean. Maybe death is their only way out of it now.

Clive's lungs burn again, but this burning precedes a numbness unlike anything he knows. As the oxygen-starved adrenaline fades, the blood cools in his veins. Water fills his lungs. He settles, stops thrashing.

The storm still rages above, and muted through the water comes another roll of thunder. The pounding of Clive's heartbeat slows enough for him to hear it.

The last thing Clive sees is Harry's lifeless face, bubbles streaming from his mouth toward the water's restless surface.

THE HANGING OF CONSTANCE EVANS

"WILL ANYONE DELIVER ME?"

Constance Evans kneeled at the edge of the stream and buried her face in her hands, sobbing. The dull amber glow washing over Salem was the most horrific sight she'd ever seen.

"Oh, holy God, have mercy upon Your daughter. Could I receive Your grace, I would repent of every wicked inkling in my soul."

The people of Salem would execute her that day on Gallows Hill, condemning her of witchcraft. As she kneeled at the water's edge and sought help from her Creator, Constance realized she was basking in her last sunrise. The realization brought on more tears.

A twig snapped, and a low voice broke from the trees. "Goody Evans, have you *no* devotion to our young Mistress, that you would seek such council from Another?"

Constance didn't have to look up to confirm the speaker. "You speak to me as though we were unfamiliar with each other."

"Constance . . . you need not resign yourself to your cruel fate so soon." Thomas Smith stepped out from the forest and got down on his knees beside her. His hand drifted over her blonde hair, tugging on it until it came loose from its braid. "At the trial, our lovely Faith promised—"

"She promised me *nothing!*" Constance twisted out of his grasp as he tried to hold her hands. "Our *lovely Faith* only further incriminated me."

"She loves you, my dear, as not even I can. Her ways are not our ways."

"You are *always* trying to justify her actions—"

He clamped a hand over her mouth, forcing her down against the grass. A sharp pain shot down her spine, but she didn't scream.

"I would be more careful with my tongue if I were you," Thomas hissed against her neck, "lest the Mistress's patience meets its end before she may deliver you."

The wind howled through the trees, lashing branch against branch. With the noise came the cold; a chill so deep and penetrating that Constance thought she'd never be warm again. A series of clouds briefly eclipsed the pale sun that rose with the wind, extinguishing natural light.

Thomas shivered and removed his hand from Constance's mouth. He took her in his arms and held her tightly as a crow cawed in the rooster's place. He was steadfast, even as her nails pricked his skin. "It is cold for September."

Constance bowed her head against his chest, muttering into the fabric of his shirt. "We should have been more careful, Thomas. After Martha Carrier's hanging . . . we should have beseeched Faith to lead us away from this place."

"You sound much like a heretic, dearest." His fingers stroked her hair away from her face. "Faith does not move unless she wishes. To suggest otherwise is blasphemy against our Mistress *and* our Master."

The blood drained from Constance's face. She lifted her chin and regarded Thomas with panic-filled eyes. "Powers and principalities forgive me. I could never hope to commit such offenses against my Prince."

"Faith will not let you perish. She will save you from your hanging."

Constance's lips narrowed into a frown, her eyes searching Thomas's desperately. She clutched his hands and held them, blinking back a tide of tears. "Would she have us *leave* tonight?"

"Her ways are not our ways," Thomas repeated. "But you have no reason to fear."

Constance sniffed and dropped her hands from Thomas's. He pulled her against him and held her. The sun climbed higher and higher into the sky. It wouldn't be long before she found herself on that dreadful hill with a rope around her neck, at the mercy of her Faith and her Master.

"Thomas," Constance said, "I love you."

"I love you too." He pressed his lips against hers. The kiss was brief and bittersweet and only made what would come to pass more terrible. Silent tears ran down Constance's cheek as Thomas pulled her to her feet and pinned her hair back up in the Puritan fashion.

"We must go now, darling, before they look for us."

Constance swallowed, took one last look at the stream, and followed her love toward Gallows Hill.

AN IMPRESSIVE CROWD HAD GATHERED TO WITNESS THE HANGING of Goody Evans. The crowd was so large, in fact, that even *Goodman* Evans had a difficult time getting close to the gallows. His daughter squeezed his hand.

"Father, let us move closer. Where we are standing now I can hardly see."

"Hush, child. The minister is about to speak."

Faith's expression darkened, but she kept silent.

THE TRICKER-TREATER AND OTHER STORIES

"We have gathered this day to observe the execution of the rampant hag, Goody Evans." The minister gestured to Constance, whom Deacon Prawley helped climb on top of a crate.

The minister cleared his throat. "This woman—the same woman who sits in our church every Sunday and partakes of the holy communion—has been tried and convicted of the cursed practice of witchcraft and of an alliance with the Prince of Darkness."

A cry of outrage arose from the crowd. Some cursed.

Constance rolled her eyes. *Hypocrites.*

The minister raised a hand to silence the crowd. His attempt only lowered the volume to a dull roar. "Her crime is an abomination before man *and* God, and for this, she will die."

Someone in the crowd screamed, "Hang the hag! Kill her! *Kill the witch!*" Others took up her cry, adding swears to the mix.

Constance shook her head, laughing to herself.

An angry villager elbowed Goodman Evans in his side. He winced.

The girl holding Goodman Evans's hand scowled at the ground. Every few seconds, she glanced up at the gallows before returning to her scowling.

Constance peered out at the crowd as Deacon Prawley slipped the noose around her neck. Thomas had assured her she had nothing to fear, that Faith would soon come to her rescue. But there didn't seem to be any reason to relax. She saw no one significant in the crowd, save for her husband, her mother, her daughter—

The noose tightened. Constance gasped.

"Goody Constance Evans," the minister intoned, "you have been tried and convicted for the dark and deceptive crime of witchcraft. You will hang by the neck until dead." He slammed his Bible closed with a thunderous *boom*. "May the Lord have mercy on your soul."

Constance remembered her feverish prayers by the stream. She bowed her head as far as the rope allowed, whimpering to herself. In calling upon the Puritan God, the God of her parents and grandparents, she had blasphemed her own Mistress. God would not save her because of her wickedness. Faith would not save her because she had spoken against Her. Constance was doomed, and she had no one to blame but herself.

Deacon Prawley kicked the crate out from underneath her feet, and she dropped like a stone in the sea.

Goodman Evans yelped as his daughter scratched his arm and jerked her hand out of his. The girl's eyes were wild and fierce, and her chest rose in quick, shallow breaths.

"Father," she growled, "get out of my way."

Goodman Evans obliged, eyes wide and unblinking as Constance's daughter shoved through the crowd, jostling and clawing her way to the gallows. She bit anyone who protested.

Darkness filled Constance's vision. A searing fire gripped her neck. She sucked at the air, but the rope sealed her throat. Blood rushed into her face. Her slowing pulse pounded in her ears.

I really am going to die, aren't I?

Distantly, a crow cawed.

No one is going to save me.

Constance's daughter leaped up onto the platform and threw Deacon Prawley to the side. When the minister dropped his Bible and ran to assist his friend, the girl hissed and kicked him in the shin. He howled in pain and toppled back against the crate.

Constance couldn't breathe.

Help me, please. Someone.

Everything's fading.

The girl hopped up on the crate and stretched her arms toward the sky. She tipped her head back to face the sun, closed her eyes, and screamed. Her scream seemed to pene-

THE TRICKER-TREATER AND OTHER STORIES

trate the fiber of every being on Gallows Hill. The grass rippled and the trees shook as though attacked by wind. Dark clouds rolled in and shut out the sun. A wave of fear unlike any she had ever known struck Constance, a fear that was blacker than black, darker than dark—a fear with a power that rattled the gates of hell. The rope securing Constance to the gallows snapped, and her body dropped to the wooden platform with a dull *thump*.

Blood rained from the sky. Women screamed and sought cover. Men tried to control their wives while trying to maintain their own composure. Deacon Prawley sprinted back to town like a man half his age, and the minister reached for his Bible but his fingers trembled so badly that he couldn't hold on to it. Constance's daughter turned on him and glared. He cried out in terror and fled the hill, the Bible forgotten.

Goodman Evans stood there for a moment, the only person left besides Constance and their daughter. He gaped at the girl as she untied the noose around his wife's neck.

"What are you looking at?" his daughter snapped. Her father stumbled backward and fell. "*Get out of here!*" *she yelled, and* Goodman Evans gasped and ran down the hill, never once stopping to see if his wife survived.

Constance lay on the unforgiving platform, reaching up to touch her bruised neck. "Wh... what happened?"

"Fool," her daughter replied. "I *delivered* you."

The bloody rain stopped, and the dark clouds rolled away to reveal the sinking sun. Realization dawned on Constance as her eyes roved over the girl's face. She fell, prostrate in conditioned submission. "Mistress! Forgive me, Faith. I never meant what I said! I was desperate—"

"*Silence.*" Faith kicked Constance in the ribs. Constance whimpered. "The only reason I saved you today was because you obeyed the Dark Prince by carrying me inside your womb for nine months. For that, He rewarded you."

"And . . . did He mention anything about permitting me to remain in this temporal state?"

"He did. You are to be transfigured into a cat again." Faith sat on the edge of the crate, swinging her legs. "After such an ordeal as this one, Father is not too convinced that you can best serve Us as a human."

Constance bit back a tide of complaint, tears welling up in her eyes once more.

"However," Faith added, "you will no longer have to hunt alone."

Thomas stepped out from the trees, smiling at Constance. He kneeled before Faith, bowing his head. "It shall please me endlessly to serve my Mistress alongside such a fair companion."

Constance's tears evaporated. "Oh, Thomas. You mean . . . ?"

"Yes, Constance. He, too, shall become a cat."

Constance smiled, unable to put her enthusiasm into words.

"Stand, Thomas." Faith raised a hand.

Thomas obeyed. Faith chanted strange, magical words that wrapped around Thomas and enclosed him in his Mistress's spell. Faith clapped her hands, raised them to the sky, and Thomas appeared again as a black cat.

"Your turn, Constance."

"Of course, Mistress. It shall be my pleasure."

Eventually, the sun set, signaling the day's end. Faith slipped into a black cloak and pulled the hood down over her eyes, leading her two followers into the woods. "Do not count this as a failure, my pets. We have not yet taken any others into communion with Our Lord, but Salem is but one village, and we have more to venture into."

Constance and Thomas padded along behind her, purring happily as mindless felines often do. Behind them, the sun gave way to the moon. A new age had begun.

CHARITY

In all his years as a priest at St. Matthew's, Father Hildebrand had never encountered anything like this before. A parishioner, Walter Harper, had died without a next of kin, and he'd asked that his possessions be donated to the church and distributed to the needy as they saw fit.

For all intents and purposes, Father Hildebrand *was* the church. He overheard confessions, performed last rites at patient deathbeds, and participated in christenings. God had called him to become a priest, and he did so gladly.

The wine cabinet sitting in front of him was large and ornate, made of dark, inlaid wood. It had a rich mahogany finish, with smooth metal latticework and a drawer built into the top—for corkscrews and such, Father Hildebrand guessed. In all honesty, he'd never been much of a drinker. Aside from the communion wine he partook in when it came time, he seldom drank, neither in his own home or even in the company of others. Alcohol had never interested him.

The cabinet, though, was beautiful. It was arguably one of the most striking things that had ever been donated. And it would be his.

A furtive glance around the room confirmed that he was the one most interested in its secrets so far. None of the other volunteers had studied it for as long as he had, not even the ones who had unloaded the piece of furniture from the van. It seemed to Father Hildebrand that the cabinet belonged to him. Perhaps God himself had made sure it would fall into his hands. After all, Walter—as far as the priest knew—had been far from a regular churchgoer. Not even the photograph of the man's face in the few dozen frames that had been dropped off had been enough to jog his memory. If the deceased parishioner had attended services and gone to confession regularly, Father Hildebrand would have known him. He knew almost everybody. That was and always had been a point of pride for him, being able to call each member of his parish by their name.

When Walter passed away, Father Hildebrand only learned his name from his attorney, the executor of the will. He'd summoned the priest for the reading and made Walter's wishes clear.

Father Hildebrand had no idea how this was supposed to go, this dividing of possessions. He'd stuck a sign out front that read FREE FURNITURE AND CLOTHES that he hoped would bring people in. Maybe there was a better way he could've worded it, but maybe it was also best to be direct.

His plan seemed to work. A few people he recognized— some churchgoers, some neighbors he'd known all his life—had trickled in to take a look at the donations. He kept his eyes on the cabinet, making sure to stake his claim as nonchalantly as he could. If anyone else wanted it, he'd have to give it to them. He couldn't be selfish, no matter how tempting. He'd have to do the right thing and make a sacrifice.

Wasn't that what Walter would have wanted him to do?

If only he'd known the man better, maybe that would have helped him here. As it stood, Father Hildebrand hoped no one

THE TRICKER-TREATER AND OTHER STORIES

else would want the cabinet. He didn't want it to go home with anyone else.

As he wandered up and down the rows of possessions, mingling with people here and there, Father Hildebrand kept his attention on the cabinet. He never outright stated that he planned to grab it, but he didn't offer it up to anyone else either. He didn't discourage anyone from picking it up, but he didn't encourage them.

For all his hard work, at the end of the day the cabinet was his to take home. A steal. Father Hildebrand was thrilled. After everyone else had cleared out, Father Hildebrand lifted the cabinet and carried it out to his SUV. He raised the hatch, folded the seats down, and strained as he wedged the cabinet into the vehicle.

It was almost too good to be true.

———

FATHER HILDEBRAND TOSSED HIS CAR KEYS IN THE BOWL BY THE door and set the cabinet down just inside the doorway. It was so heavy it made grooves in the shag carpet. Panting, he wiped a sheen of sweat from his brow. His back hurt something awful. He was supposed to lift with his knees, but in the excitement of nabbing the cabinet he'd forgotten proper form. He'd pay for that tomorrow, when he woke up sore and cranky. It used to be that it didn't matter how improperly he'd lifted or carried something, his muscles always bounced back. Now, it was another story.

Maybe he was getting old. Or maybe he'd gotten old already and somehow hadn't noticed. He didn't know which was worse.

Once he caught his breath, Father Hildebrand surveyed his home. Where should he put the cabinet? Its size made it difficult to wedge between his existing furniture. It almost needed its own space, propped against the wall. It was certainly more than worthy of that.

He looked around. Framed photographs of his church and parishioners hung on the wall by the door, sharing space with an entry table and a glass bowl filled with keys. A thrift-store lamp sat at the end of the table. That wall was out of the question.

There was a half-wall and a bar between the living room and the kitchen, but the cabinet would come up past the bar. That wouldn't work either.

He could put it in the bedroom, which was sparse in terms of furniture and decor, but it seemed a crime to hide such a lovely thing away. It needed to be one of the first things people saw when they entered his house. The hallway leading to the bedroom and the bathroom was empty, but it didn't belong there. The shadows would swallow it. No, he had to find a spot for it in the living room, somewhere it could be the focal point.

Father Hildebrand looked at his couch. Like most everything in his home, it sagged and creaked in places. The sunlight that streamed in through the front windows had faded the rich coffee color to a dull, brownish gray. Still, he couldn't part with it. The couch had been his first purchase upon becoming a priest at St. Matthew's. Its sentimental value made up for its eyesore nature.

The shag carpet was another story. It was ugly for no reason.

Sighing, Father Hildebrand grabbed the wobbly end table and dragged it to the side. He hated to put the cabinet next to the couch, but it made the most sense there. He didn't intend to use it like he used the end table, but he supposed he could if he wanted to. It just seemed too opulent to have a coaster and a mug placed on top of it.

He looked back at the wine cabinet. Its luster and lattice-work thrilled him. Would it hurt to purchase some wine bottles for it? It seemed like such a shame not to use the object to its full potential. As for the drawer . . . well, he had a corkscrew somewhere, didn't he? He could go and put that in there, make the cabinet feel more *his*.

Father Hildebrand wiped his face again. Maybe he needed a new window unit. The one in his bedroom wasn't enough to cool the whole house, and he couldn't stop sweating. Maybe he was just more out of shape than he'd expected.

He went back to the cabinet, hunched against it, and carefully pushed it into place. It fit the groove left by the end table nicely, like it had been made to replace it. Father Hildebrand straightened it and stepped back to admire his handiwork. Yes, a few wine bottles would fit nicely in the top of the cabinet, tucked into the iron lattice. Cabernet Sauvignon, Malbec, Pinot Grigio . . . he liked them all well enough, but even if he didn't drink them, they would look good displayed there. As for the drawer, he had to go get that corkscrew.

Although Father Hildebrand's knees and back screamed at him to sit, he went into the kitchen and rummaged through the drawers there until he found what he was looking for. It turned out he had two corkscrews, gifts from parishioners he hadn't brought himself to throw out. They would look perfect nestled in the wine cabinet. He brought them over to his latest acquisition, humming as he braced a hand against the wood's smooth finish. He set the corkscrews down and pulled open the drawer.

A hellish scream tore from inside the cabinet. Father Hildebrand staggered backward. A gaunt, pale entity rose from the door and stretched toward the ceiling. Its essence was milky white, almost transparent; its eyes were the color of blood. They burned in the house's dim lighting as they settled on the priest. The creature stretched a ragged claw toward him.

Father Hildebrand yelled and jumped back from the entity's reach. He backed against the wall and cowered, clutching the cross on the chain around his neck. He was halfway through a fervent prayer when the creature sought him again.

"Father," it bellowed in a reedy, raspy voice. "You are not the owner of this cabinet."

Father Hildebrand's vision tunneled. What if he fainted? What would the entity do to him then? He gaped, wide-eyed, and struggled to come up with a response. "I . . . well, I am now. The owner . . . passed away."

The creature blinked its giant eyes and let its claw fall by its side. It had no legs, its form just dissipated into tendrils of fog at the waist. Its gaze made Father Hildebrand's eyes water. He had to look away.

"He left it to you?" the creature asked.

"Well, he . . . more or less." The sharp edges of the cross bit Father Hildebrand's palm. He ignored the pain. "He wanted his possessions left to the church. To be parceled out at . . . the church's discretion."

The creature hummed. It said nothing for a painful stretch of time, and fear crept over Father Hildebrand's heart and trickled into his stomach. Panic roiled in his gut. Whatever this thing was, it had the potential to hurt him. Why it hadn't yet was anyone's guess. Maybe he had something it wanted?

"Can . . . can I do anything to help you?" Father Hildebrand prompted. He forced himself to look into the creature's face again, directing his attention at its forehead this time so as not to hurt himself. "I help people for a living, you see. It's my calling. If there's something you need help with, something you'd like me to do . . . well, I'm more than happy to do it."

Maybe appealing to the creature and submitting to its whims would soothe it. Father Hildebrand could only hope it knew he was sincere, not just putting on an act to save his skin —although maybe there was some truth to that part.

"I'm a ghost," the entity said.

"All right, well, what do you want with me?"

"It's better if I show you." The ghost leered at him. At least, he *thought* it leered. It was hard to tell since it didn't have a mouth. Then it lunged at Father Hildebrand. He had just enough time to raise his cross up by his face before the ghost slammed into him and the priest's whole world went dark.

————

WHEN FATHER HILDEBRAND CAME TO, HIS MOUTH WAS FULL OF cotton. At least, it felt that way. His whole head felt swollen and too big for his body. His throat burned, his bones ached. Part of him felt like screaming, although he didn't know why.

Mostly, he felt hungover, but he'd never been hungover in his life.

"Good," came a voice in his head. "You're awake."

Father Hildebrand started. He pulled his knees to his chest and hugged them close to his body. "Who's there? In the name of the Lord—"

"That won't work with me. Sorry." The raspiness reminded Father Hildebrand of the ghost, and it all came flooding back to him. The ghost's voice was in his head. "You're wondering where I am, right?"

Father Hildebrand looked around the room. His corkscrews were on the floor and the wine cabinet drawer was still open, but everything else looked normal. "I can hear you, but I don't see you."

"I possessed you, Father. That's where I am now." A twinge caught the back of his neck, making Father Hildebrand gasp. "I'm pulling the strings."

"You hurt me," Father Hildebrand said.

"I didn't. I can, but I'm hoping you won't make me. I'm hoping you can give me exactly what I want."

The ghost squeezed Father Hildebrand's stomach, and he groaned, pressing a hand against the wall for support. This was not how he'd thought his evening would go. He never would have taken the cabinet home if he'd known this would happen.

Could it be that his parishioner had known something like this would happen? Did Walter know the ghost had been lying in wait for some poor soul?

Father Hildebrand winced. The creature's impatience flared up inside him. It was waiting for his response.

"Why do you need me?" Father Hildebrand asked.

"I need a body to do what I want. Yours just happened to be the closest and most convenient vessel." He felt the ghost sneer at him. "I'm hurt that you don't recognize me."

Father Hildebrand blanched. "You're . . . someone I should know?"

"A former member of your flock, Father. The one who left you the cabinet."

A flicker of realization washed through the priest. "You're Walter."

"That's correct."

"Why did you ask me where the cabinet came from, then? If you already knew."

"I had to make sure my wishes had been carried out." The ghost pulled Father Hildebrand's hand off the wall. "I had a feeling I'd end up in the drawer. I wanted to be put in capable hands."

Father Hildebrand frowned. "If I hadn't brought the cabinet home, where would you be now?"

"I would've gotten someone else to help me. But I tried everything I could to draw your eyes to the cabinet. I enhanced the wood's luster. I made the piece shine. Father, I wanted you to be the one to help me. You've helped me before, in so many ways and without ever knowing. I need your help again."

As Father Hildebrand absorbed the ghost's words—*Walter's* words—a strange guilt settled over him. He hadn't done enough for this man while he'd been living. He hadn't even recognized Walter, hadn't remembered him, yet he'd had such a profound effect on his life? What did that say about him, that he could forget the ones whose lives he'd touched?

"Oh, Father," Walter murmured. "It isn't your fault. Nothing you did put me in this situation. But you can help get me out of it. Will you listen to my plight?"

"I could exorcise you," Father Hildebrand said. "Or, well, I could try to. I'm . . . I'm out of practice, and I've only tried it once, but I could do it. I could. I could cast you out of me."

"Maybe you could. Most likely you couldn't. Do you really want to risk that? Making me angry?"

To prove his point, Walter twisted Father Hildebrand's ankle. Father Hildebrand cried out, pain arcing up his calf as he lunged forward and caught himself on the edge of the couch. He spoke through ragged breaths. "I can't help you if you hurt me."

"Which is why I don't want to," Walter said. "Hear me out. Help me. I swear, I'll be good."

Father Hildebrand thought for a moment. It was his duty, his calling as a member of the clergy, to help anyone who needed it. This creature—Walter—had come to him with a problem, and if he didn't try to solve it, he'd be going against his calling. Against God's purpose for him.

Whatever Walter wanted, Father Hildebrand couldn't refuse. His soul hung in the balance.

"All right, I'll help you, Walter. Tell me what you need."

———

WALTER DROVE FATHER HILDEBRAND'S SUV TO THE OTHER SIDE of town. They pulled into a neighborhood with a sign that read SHADY HILLS. As Walter relaxed his hold on the priest, Father Hildebrand tightened his grip on the steering wheel. It felt bizarre to share his body with someone he barely knew. It unsettled him, to say the least,

"Do you remember the poem?" Walter prompted in his head.

"I . . . I'll write it down," Father Hildebrand said. "Just let me know when we're close to her house. I'll pull over, you can tell me again, and this time I'll write it down."

Walter settled a little. His relief warmed Father Hildebrand. "I hope she's still where I think she is. How long has it been since I died?"

"Not long. You've been in the ground about a week, I think. You didn't look her up before?"

"No. I never thought to. Guess I thought I'd have more time." Walter hummed. "Guess everybody thinks that."

Father Hildebrand nodded for want of anything wise to say. Since Walter's death, he'd thought little about his own mortality. He hadn't been the one to conduct the funeral, otherwise he might have reflected on the matter at hand much more. He wasn't sure why he was the one being possessed if someone else had done the funeral, but that was another story. It didn't matter now. All that mattered was that he had to get this poem to Walter's long-lost love and complete his unfinished business so Walter could move on and go to heaven.

It bothered Father Hildebrand that he'd gotten the afterlife wrong. Nothing in the Bible corresponded with Walter's experience. He'd never believed in ghosts, never taught his parishioners that it was something that they could turn into. Had he inadvertently led them astray with his ignorance? *Lord, please forgive me*, he prayed. What was it the Bible said? *Whosoever causes a man to stumble . . .*

"Father," Walter said. "It wasn't your fault. Nobody knows they'll turn into a ghost."

Father Hildebrand choked back his embarrassment at being overheard praying. "That was supposed to be a private act. You told me you thought it might happen. You had an idea. How did you know?"

"I had unfinished business. When I got sick, I thought about her. I thought about Agnes and everything left unsaid." Walter's sigh rumbled in Father Hildebrand's chest. "My neighbor . . . a single mother, she warned me—I didn't listen. I told her I believed in heaven and hell, so it didn't matter. I'd go to one of those."

"We know so little," Father Hildebrand said. "Human beings. Don't we?"

As if reading his mind, sensing his anguish, Walter sighed again. "You do the best you can, Father. No one expects you to have all the answers. You do know that, don't you?"

He did, somehow. Of course he did. But it was nice hearing someone else say it. Too often Father Hildebrand busied himself reassuring others when he himself so desperately needed reassurance himself. Walter's words soothed his nerves. He relaxed his grip on the steering wheel and tried to focus on the present, on what he had agreed to do.

"Thank you," Father Hildebrand said.

"It's the least I can do. Turn right at the stop sign."

Father Hildebrand appreciated that Walter let him drive now instead of taking over like he had done before. Maybe Walter trusted him more now that they'd opened up to each other. Maybe Walter realized that he had no choice but to trust Father Hildebrand. After all, there was no one else who could help him now.

Following Walter's instructions, Father Hildebrand flipped on his indicator and took a right at the next stop sign. Shrubs and trees lined the sleepy neighborhood streets, and sidewalks stretched in front of houses as far as the eye could see. Presumably, no homeowner's association ruled over the neighborhood —no two houses looked the same, and some of the lawns were overgrown.

"She grew up here?" Father Hildebrand asked.

"Yeah. We were neighbors. Best friends," Walter said. "She was my first love. Should've been my last. If only . . ."

Father Hildebrand waited for Walter to continue, but he

never finished his thought. Instead, it trailed off into the ether and the silence of the car. The hum of the engine made the silence tolerable. Father Hildebrand had more questions, but he wasn't sure they were relevant, and Walter's anxiety crowded him. He felt the ghost's nerves taking over his emotions.

"Why are you so nervous?" Father Hildebrand asked. "Forgive me, but . . . you're dead. You've passed on. There isn't any risk here, is there?"

Walter hesitated. Father Hildebrand wondered what he was thinking—if ghosts could even think. He still knew next to nothing about him.

"Once you give her the poem, my business is finished," Walter said. "As long as you fulfill your end of the bargain . . . no, there's no risk. It doesn't matter what comes next. But . . ." He faltered for a minute, searching for the right words, if the priest had to guess. "I would like some resolution. Closure. I hope that's not too much to ask."

"You'll get it," Father Hildebrand said.

"Maybe that's what I'm afraid of. Right now, what's left of my future is open. This is the last thing I have left on Earth. After all this is over, I have to move on."

"And if she says no, if she doesn't reciprocate . . . ?"

"I'll have to dwell on that regret for an eternity." Walter's sorrow blanketed Father Hildebrand's consciousness, and tears pricked his eyes. He couldn't imagine what Walter was feeling, the true extent of it, even though he had a glimpse.

"It's human to want closure, and it's human to be scared." Father Hildebrand swallowed the lump that had risen in his throat. "Bravery is moving forward regardless of your fear. That's something to admire."

"Thank you, Father Hildebrand. Turn left here. Be careful, I remember a blind drive somewhere nearby. Could be tricky."

Father Hildebrand followed Walter's instructions. The ghost's trepidation mounted as they got closer to their final destination. His nerves tugged at the loose threads of Father Hildebrand's own. Though he knew he was doing the right thing in helping Walter move on, Father Hildebrand had to admit he'd be glad to see the ghost gone. He wanted to feel at home in his body again.

"What do you think she'll say?" Father Hildebrand asked.

"I don't know," Walter said. "That's what scares me more than anything."

They turned right again and came up on a speed limit sign announcing Father Hildebrand was driving too fast. He couldn't help it. Walter's nervousness had rubbed off on him, and Father Hildebrand would be lying if he said he wasn't ready to be rid of the ghost. Still, he eased up on the accelerator. He kept his eyes peeled, his body alert, scanning each mailbox they passed for lucky number 1105.

"We must be close now," Walter said.

"Why can't you just take over? Recite the poem yourself." Father Hildebrand braked to avoid hitting a squirrel. "That way, you'll be sure it comes across how you intended."

"It takes an incredible amount of energy just to communicate with you, and that's all internally and without much emotion," Walter said. "No offense. To recite a whole poem to the woman I love . . . well, you get the picture."

Father Hildebrand nodded. As loathe as he was to admit it, Walter's argument made sense. And as reluctant as he was to put himself out there for two complete strangers, it had to be done. Once he'd finished his task, he'd be free again.

But would he ever be the same after this encounter? He doubted it. Father Hildebrand had no clue what he'd do differently once Walter left him, but he couldn't keep the incident to himself. He'd have to tell someone.

His mind flashed back to their earlier conversation about the afterlife. As a priest, Father Hildebrand preached about heaven and hell and purgatory, but all of that happened beyond Earth, *beyond* the material plane. That was what he preached and what he believed in. But then Walter had come along. Now, Father Hildebrand wasn't sure what he believed. He couldn't in good conscience tell his parish what he'd always told them, not when he'd witnessed evidence that he didn't have all the answers.

Father Hildebrand cleared his throat. "Do you know anyone else this has happened to? That is, can you see other people in your circumstance?"

"Other ghosts? Entities?"

"Yes."

"No," Walter said. "There's no one here but me. If anyone else is running around trying to get unsuspecting priests to do their bidding, I can't see them. And no one else is bothering you."

"Hm."

"Sorry to disappoint you. I'm not thrilled about it either. I hate being alone."

"You're not alone. You have me."

"You know what I mean." Walter's excitement flared in Father Hildebrand's head, dizzying him. "Yellow house at the end of the cul-de-sac. Slowly."

Per Walter's urging, Father Hildebrand let off the gas. He started to brake, but Walter seized his foot and pressed the pedal all the way down until the car stopped. Walter directed Father Hildebrand's hand to the gearshift and put the car in park.

"Having second thoughts?" Father Hildebrand asked.

"I'm sorry. I shouldn't have taken over like that," Walter said. "I just . . . it all feels too real now. There's no going back. Maybe this wouldn't be such a big deal if I were still alive, but with this being my unfinished business and all that . . . it just feels so final. I know once this is finished, all of it is finished. All of me. And . . . that's hard to come to terms with."

Father Hildebrand nodded. Although he'd never died and had never been a ghost, he could empathize with Walter. His empathy had led him to become a priest, after all. If he couldn't even show a nonhuman entity a bit of humanity, his calling was in vain.

"I had a crush on a girl when I was thirteen," Father Hildebrand said. "Her name was Molly. She seemed like a good Catholic girl, the kind my parents would have loved for me to marry. But she had a wild streak. Few people saw it. No one was supposed to eavesdrop on confessions, but I heard her say such dirty things. I couldn't help myself. I found every excuse to linger outside the booth, mostly on the pretense of going in next. I think she knew I was there. I think she . . ." He licked his lips. "I think she said those things on purpose."

"Not my Agnes," Walter said. "She's a good girl through and through. A respectable woman."

"I've met respectable women. You'd be surprised."

"What's that supposed to mean?"

"I'm just saying, maybe you should manage your expectations. It's been a long time since you've seen her, right? People change."

Walter's anger simmered under the surface of Father Hildebrand's consciousness. "Jesus, Father, don't hold back. You're supposed to be helping me fulfill my last wish. It doesn't matter how you feel about it, but I'd prefer you be supportive. It's so much easier if you're on my side."

"Yeah, well, forgive me for not feeling too charitable. You've possessed me." Of his own volition, the priest scratched the back of his neck. "All etiquette has more or less gone out the window."

"Is that how God would have you treat me?"

Father Hildebrand bristled. "You have no idea of God's will. You can't understand it. To say otherwise is blasphemy, and you know that's unforgivable."

"I'm already dead," Walter said. "Already cursed. I don't think it can get much worse for me."

His words pricked Father Hildebrand's spine. More than anything, he wanted to brush Walter off. He didn't want to let his speech or attitude get to him, but . . . maybe he had a point. The afterlife was already shaping up to be entirely different from what Father Hildebrand had expected. How many more surprises were in store?

It was folly—and sin—to claim to know God's will. But it was also a sin to think there wasn't more beyond death than what he preached, especially when he'd been presented with undeniable evidence to the contrary.

"What are you thinking?" Walter asked.

"You can't read my thoughts?" Father Hildebrand mused.

"No, and if I could, I still wouldn't. It's rude."

"Ruder than taking control of my body? Harassing a clergyman?"

"Pleading the Fifth. Answer me, please."

Father Hildebrand stared at their intended destination: the small yellow house. What was it like to have your life's goal within reach? To have the potential to achieve what you'd only dreamed about? As difficult as it was to feel sorry for Walter, he could understand his motivation. And, he had to admit, if he were in Walter's shoes, he'd probably be struggling too.

"I'm . . . conflicted," Father Hildebrand said. "I do want to help you, but you're wearing me down. I don't know how this woman, Agnes, is going to react to a stranger reciting a poem, let alone proclaiming his love for her when he's a vessel for a dead man she knew as a girl. I want to do the right thing. I want to be charitable, gracious . . . but I don't know how, exactly. This situation isn't one I've prepared for."

Walter sighed. His anger rolled into resignation. "I appreciate your help so far. I know this can't be easy. I know I'm asking a lot of someone who doesn't even remember seeing me in his church."

Father Hildebrand winced. It was true. He couldn't deny it. As much as he wanted to reassure Walter that he remembered him, he didn't. Their initial interaction had made that clear, and even as he racked his brain for a memory of the man to latch on to, he couldn't come up with anything. Guilt struck him like a blow.

"I wish I had known you better, Walter. I really do. I'm sorry."

"That's nice of you to say, even if I don't believe it." Walter sighed again. "Maybe I shouldn't stall anymore. We have work to do, right? One last task and you'll be rid of me. I'm sure you can't wait."

"I'd like my body back, for sure."

"Let's get this over with, then."

Walter put Father Hildebrand's hand back on the gearshift and put the car in drive. Pressing his lips together, Father Hildebrand waited for Walter to take his foot off the brake. He tried to be patient.

Still, Walter hesitated. "Do you think this is wise?"

Father Hildebrand wanted to say yes, but it wouldn't matter, would it? He doubted anything he could say would deter Walter from moving forward, but he at least wanted to tell him the truth. Even a ghost deserved that much from him.

"I don't, I'm afraid. I don't know what good could come of it."

Instead of angry, Walter's tone was bereft. "I think you're right. But if I don't try, I can't move on. I need to move on, Father. I need to go to heaven, or wherever the next stop is."

"Right," said Father Hildebrand. "Okay, then. Let's do it."

Without Walter's prodding or intervention, Father Hildebrand put his foot on the gas and pulled the car into the driveway of the yellow house. It was poured concrete, cracked in some places, with weeds poking out of those fissures. A large oil stain marred the surface until the SUV covered it. He put the vehicle back in park and sat for a minute, letting the engine idle.

"Can we try the poem again?" Walter asked.

Father Hildebrand's tongue darted out to wet his lips. He shut his eyes and recited the poem:

> *"Drink to me only with thine eyes,*
> *And I will pledge with mine;*
> *Or leave a kiss but in the cup,*
> *And I'll not look for wine.*
> *The thirst that from the soul doth rise*
> *Doth ask a drink divine;*
> *But might I of Jove's nectar sup,*
> *I would not change for thine.*
>
> *I sent thee late a rosy wreath,*
> *Not so much honouring thee*
> *As giving it a hope, that there*
> *It could not withered be.*
> *But thou thereon didst only breathe,*
> *And sent'st it back to me;*
> *Since when it grows, and smells, I swear,*
> *Not of itself, but thee."*

Walter's approval bloomed like a flower and flooded Father Hildebrand's veins with warmth. The sensation was so foreign it made Father Hildebrand's skin itch. He scratched at his arms.

"Isn't that lovely?" Walter asked. "Your memory is better than I thought."

"I'm fifty-three," Father Hildebrand said. "I don't think my mind should be going just yet. Besides, you made me read it seven times, remember?"

"That's right. I'd nearly forgotten." Walter's tone turned wistful. "Now, if you're ready, we can proceed."

Father Hildebrand wanted to ask Walter if *he* was ready, but it didn't matter anymore. They'd come too far. They couldn't turn back now. All he had to do was turn the car off, get out, go up to the door, and knock. His memory and God would take care of the rest.

They got out of the car and headed up the steps to Agnes's front door. It was red, faded from the sun, with peeling paint along the edges. A potted plant with flowers sat beside the door. Father Hildebrand knew nothing about plants.

"This is it," Walter said. "Knock on the door. Go on."

"Easy for you to say," Father Hildebrand muttered. He could make a fool of himself in front of a stranger. Meanwhile, Walter stood to lose nothing. He was already dead.

Father Hildebrand raised his fist and froze. What if he got the poem wrong? What if the woman thought he'd lost his mind? What if she called the police?

He glanced back at his SUV sitting in the driveway. It wasn't too late to turn back after all, was it? Not when he could turn tail and run and Walter couldn't do a thing about it.

Then again, it was his duty to help his parishioners. His *calling*. He had to follow through with this act of charity or risk somehow incurring God's wrath.

"Father," Walter prompted.

Father Hildebrand went to knock again, but something stilled his hand. A bird called out. Walter bumped up against his consciousness again, his frustration bubbling to the surface. Before he could protest, Father Hildebrand pushed through his mental block and knocked. Muffled voices echoed from inside the home. He drew back from the door and contemplated stepping away, but Walter propelled him forward again. This time, his frustration was impossible to ignore.

"You've already knocked. She must have heard you. Can't get out of this one now, Father."

"I could," Father Hildebrand argued. "I could leave."

"But that goes against your calling to help those in need, doesn't it?" Walter oozed smugness. Father Hildebrand knew he'd lost. "You don't want to help me, but you must."

Father Hildebrand sighed. He was ready to knock again when the door swung inward to reveal a woman much older than him, presumably around Walter's age. Her eyes crinkled at the corners as she smiled.

"Can I help you, Father?"

He was glad he'd worn his collar. It would maybe make things easier. Nervousness squeezed his throat and he had to clear it to reply. "Are you . . . is your name Agnes, ma'am?"

"It's her," Walter said. "I'd stake my life on it."

"Too late for that," Father Hildebrand muttered.

"I'm sorry?" the woman asked.

"Nothing, my apologies." He tried again, gentler this time. "I have a message for Agnes. To whom am I speaking?"

"It's her," Walter repeated.

Her smile faded, turned wary. Her eyes narrowed. "That's me."

"She's more beautiful than I remember," Walter said. He sounded far away and dreamlike. "I shouldn't have let my opportunity pass. Look at her. Just look."

"I'm Father Hildebrand," he said. "And the message is from Walter. Walter, um . . ."

"Harper!" Walter's shout made him wince.

"Walter Harper!" His face reddened. He'd yelled the name like a curse. "So sorry. Did you know that he passed?"

"Walter Harper." The smile vanished altogether. Her eyebrows drew together. "I'd . . . I'd heard, yes. Afraid I couldn't attend the funeral. My grandson . . ."

Father Hildebrand gave her a moment alone with her grief

and didn't prompt her to finish her sentence. So far, the situation didn't have the right tone for what Walter wanted him to say. He couldn't see how to transition from this conversation to one about love, one where it made sense for a complete stranger to recite a poem to her on behalf of her dead friend.

"What are you waiting for?" Walter asked. "Do it."

The ghost wasn't too skilled at reading the room. If it were up to Father Hildebrand, he'd end everything right there. Fire off a quick apology, offer condolences, and leave. But of course, it wasn't up to Father Hildebrand to decide what happened next. It wasn't up to Walter. It was all up to God.

God was the one who'd gotten him into this mess, after all. He was the one who'd called Father Hildebrand to serve him.

He never said anything about helping a ghost, though, did he? And he didn't say a thing about reciting poems to a stranger.

Father Hildebrand sighed again. He wrung his hands. His heart pounded. "Would you . . . could I share something with you, Agnes? It's something Walter wanted you to hear."

Agnes's hand went to her hip. Something bulged in her pocket, but she shifted to the side before Father Hildebrand could see it. If it was possible, her eyes narrowed even further as she looked the priest over.

"Walter Harper, you said." It wasn't a question. Her change in tone rang alarm bells in his head. Maybe he shouldn't—

"Let me do it," Walter said.

Father Hildebrand bristled. "I thought you said it took up too much energy."

Agnes, still with her hand on her hip, looked at him with wariness behind her caramel eyes. He didn't blame her. He was a strange man on her front porch, talking to himself and claiming to know someone she'd grown up with. He was surprised she still wanted to listen to him. If he were her, he probably would have kicked him off her porch.

The sooner they got out of there, the better. It was time for Walter's poem.

"Go on," Walter prompted. "Before you lose your nerve."

And the sooner he recited the poem, the sooner he'd be free of Walter forever.

Father Hildebrand's tongue darted out to wet his lips. He cleared his throat. He started.

"Drink to me only with thine eyes,
And I will pledge with mine;
Or leave a kiss but in the cup,
And I'll not look for wi—"

Agnes whipped a knife out of her pocket and stabbed Father Hildebrand in the stomach. He cried out, doubling over as Agnes pulled the knife back out and raised it again. The second time, it caught him in the shoulder. He screamed.

"Call an ambulance," he groaned.

Agnes stabbed him in the chest, right under his collar. Blood dripped from the puncture and streamed down his stomach when she pulled the knife out again.

The horizon tilted and Father Hildebrand's vision tunneled. He dropped to his knees. The air whooshed out of his lungs in a pained gasp. He'd *known*. Somehow, just before he'd knocked on the door, he'd known this was going to happen.

Not this exactly, but still.

Father Hildebrand caught himself with his hand before his face hit the decking. He lay on his stomach, blood oozing in a warm pool underneath him. In a way, it was poetic. It was like God had willed it.

Agnes stepped away from him. Her knife clattered to the porch. Father Hildebrand had to crane his neck to look at her. Although her face was stony, tears shone in her eyes. Maybe . . . she was smiling. Maybe just a little.

His vision darkened. It was hard to focus on what was happening anymore.

"Walter," Father Hildebrand murmured. If all of this had been part of some twisted plan, he deserved an explanation. "Walter, please, what's . . . what's happening?"

Agnes's labored breathing caught his ears instead. Walter remained silent. Father Hildebrand had asked Agnes to call an ambulance, but she hadn't moved. Her hands fluttered at her sides, twitching like dying birds.

He had to get help or he was going to die, no two ways about it. He had to call a doctor.

Something hard scraped against his hipbone as he rolled onto his side. His cellphone. If he could just get to it now, if it had service, he could dial 911.

"Agnes, grab the phone." The words came from Father Hildebrand's mouth, but they belonged to Walter. His voice burst out again like vomit. "He's going for the phone."

Agnes lunged forward and bent over the priest. He twisted away but she held him steady, straddling him with a speed that defied her age. It was the closest the priest had been to a woman in ages, but that was the last thing on his mind now.

"Walter," Agnes hissed. "Where is it?"

"Right pocket. I'll try to hold him."

Father Hildebrand wanted to scream, but the sound bubbled in his chest and stayed there. Every breath hurt. Every second ticking by felt like sand through his fingers. If he didn't find a way out, he wouldn't make it to his car. He wouldn't make it anywhere ever again.

Agnes stuck her bony hand down his pocket and fumbled for the phone. He lacked the strength to fight her. How much of that was blood loss, and how much was Walter? It all melted together.

"Got it." Agnes got to her feet and brushed herself off, as though being near Father Hildebrand had soiled her. She studied the phone before slipping it into her own pocket. "Anyone know he was here?"

"No," Walter said with Father Hildebrand's voice. "No one."

Muffled voices echoed out from inside again. Maybe someone else was in there, someone who could call for help. Someone who could save his life.

Father Hildebrand opened his mouth to call out—

"*And that's why I only trust Tide in my house. Nothing but the best for my family.*" The tinny jingle of a commercial rang hollow in the priest's ears. Of course, he should've known. It was just the television.

Walter trembled inside Father Hildebrand, pushing and prodding against his body and spreading heat and pain through his limbs.

"What made you hurt me?" Father Hildebrand asked. He almost didn't expect an answer. None of it mattered anymore. He would bleed out nonetheless.

"Walter found me weeks ago," Agnes said. "He knew he was going to die, had a feeling. And . . . he wanted me to know how he'd felt all the years." Despite their grim circumstances, she smiled. "So romantic. He pledged he'd find a way for us to be together, even if he passed."

Pain bloomed in Father Hildebrand's gut and blossomed up into his chest. He cried out again. Maybe he shouldn't have asked. None of this changed anything.

"This . . . was his plan?" Father Hildebrand asked. "He wanted to possess me . . . and bring me here to you?"

Agnes nodded. "He needed a willing vessel, someone who *had* to help him. And, Father, you were perfect. You were called to help people like him. You couldn't refuse, or else you'd risk divine retribution. That's when Walter decided."

Father Hildebrand's limbs tingled, filled with pins and needles. His head swam. Halfheartedly, he pressed his hand against the knife wound in his stomach and applied pressure as best he could. The pain mocked him.

"How did he know I'd take the cabinet?"

"He didn't, but you did. That's the act that sealed your fate."

Almost all the fight left Father Hildebrand's body. He struggled to remember the last rites, what he was supposed to say, any sins he wanted to confess before he shuffled off the mortal coil. He came up empty everywhere.

"Why?" Father Hildebrand asked.

"Why what?" Agnes said.

"Why do you two . . . want me dead?"

For the first time since he'd met her, Agnes's face softened. "Walter didn't tell you? He . . . he needs your body, see. Once you're dead, your soul leaves, and you're just an empty vessel. Someone else—Walter—can fill that. Take over, as it were."

Sick realization washed over Father Hildebrand. Nausea roiled in his bleeding stomach. Any kindness Walter had shown him, any glimpse of warmth—it had been just that, a *glimpse*. A ruse. All calculated to get Father Hildebrand to do exactly what he and Agnes wanted.

Father Hildebrand's act of charity had gotten him stabbed and killed, bleeding out on an old woman's porch. He'd been an old fool, after all.

Agnes kneeled beside him. Father Hildebrand struggled to see past the darkness encroaching on his vision, but he recognized her perfume. She smelled like sweat and gardenias. Her hand slipped under the back of his head as she eased his torso onto her lap.

"Does it hurt too much?" she asked.

Odd that she'd care about his well-being now. Father Hildebrand groaned. "He . . . how can Walter use my body if it's riddled with stab wounds?"

His eyes fell shut as Agnes rubbed his back, almost like his mother had when he was a child. "The soul transfer heals them. It'll be like you're brand new."

Not me, Father Hildebrand thought. *Not me, but Walter.*

The numbness took over his body, making any movement impossible. Not much time left, then. Not much time left to do anything at all but beg for God's forgiveness and curse Walter, if he could.

"I'll take care of your flock," Walter said. Father Hildebrand wished he had the strength to scream.

His body shuddered. Hard. He couldn't open his eyes.

"I know the last rites, Father. I'll do them for you." Agnes's voice again. An unexpected blessing. Some strange part of him wanted to thank her, even after what she'd done.

"Goodbye," Walter murmured.

Goodbye.

THE SESSION

THE THERAPIST'S OFFICE LOOKED OUT OVER THE PARK. GOLD
curtains framed the windows, the ends grazing the oat-colored
shag carpet. The room was spartan; the only things that lived
there were a handful of chairs, a desk, a bookcase, and a potted
plant. Aging wood paneling covered the walls. To Sheila, the
good view didn't make up for the room's oppressive vibe. She
looked at Dirk and sat, her body cramped in the faux-leather
chair.

"I've heard of you two." The therapist's blonde hair did not
move as she adjusted her bun. "I don't know anyone who hasn't.
You're seeking therapy for what you went through?"

Sheila twisted the white-gold band on her finger. Although
Dirk had taken his ring off, she felt naked without hers. "This
isn't about the island. It's about an affair."

Dirk scratched his stubble. "It's about our whole marriage."

"I see." The therapist scribbled something and tapped her
pen against her cheek. "Why don't you tell me about it?"

"A week ago, I walked in on him having sex with someone
else." Sheila pulled her hair into a ponytail. She had to keep her
hands busy so she wouldn't bite her cuticles. Her fingertips

69

were already covered with polka-dot Band-Aids. "We've only been back for two months. How could this have happened?"

"Did you ask him about it?"

Sheila clenched her fists. "Of course I asked him. Why wouldn't I have?"

Dirk bumped Sheila's knee with his. "You need to get some air?"

Sheila's nails dug into her thighs. She stood and smoothed her skirt. "I'd like a drink of water."

While the therapist poured her a glass from the pitcher, Sheila thought about water. They had *worshiped* water on the island. The first few days, she'd laid on the sand with the sun beating down, begging for Dirk to kill her so she wouldn't die of thirst. He'd asked her when she wanted him to do it. *Be certain, dear.*

The therapist handed Sheila the glass. She drank the whole thing down. Dirk set the empty cup on the table for her. Did *he* remember the water? Did he remember how it felt to be so thirsty?

"Go back a little," the therapist said. "When did you first notice something was amiss?"

Amiss. Like their marriage was a painting hanging crooked on the wall. Sheila stared at the glass on the table. She'd always known they'd get a divorce. As high school sweethearts, their chances of growing old together were slim. Going into the marriage, both had known that. Still, they had tried. For the sake of their unborn child, they had tried.

If Sheila closed her eyes, she still felt the wedding dress clinging to her stomach. She remembered the smell of roses and the soft organ music. Her mind flashed ahead to the blood in the bathtub.

Her stomach lurched.

"We were doing all right until we lost the baby," Dirk said. There was no need for him to elaborate. The therapist had their file. What she did not know was how the island had repaired them. She did not know that the day they found water was the day they made love, for the first time in months. She had no idea that Sheila was pregnant again. Neither did Dirk.

"Sheila," Dirk said, "are you sure you're all right?"

"I was all right, Dirk. I was doing fine until you brought that slut home."

His jaw tightened. "You know that's not the only issue we're here for. We had problems way before Cassandra."

Cassandra. She knew the woman's name, but the sound of it rolled around inside her mind again. She could feel the weight of it on her tongue. It tasted bitter and metallic, like blood oozing from cracked lips. She had learned to like the taste of blood on the island. After days of dry mouth, the wetness of blood on the tip of her tongue relieved her. Even now, she could taste it. Sometimes she even missed it. She missed it right then. On the island, Dirk had pressed his fingers to her mouth. "I wish I could save us," he had said. His lips brushed hers, rough on rough, but it was only a memory. Had he kissed her since then?

"We haven't had sex since the island," Sheila said. "At first, I thought he didn't feel up to it. I quit initiating. Then I came home from work and found out it's nothing with him. He just doesn't want me."

She had her students help her make a love collage. Second-graders, prone to distraction on their own, became ultra-focused when given a goal. With Sheila's supervision, they cut out pictures of hearts and happy couples. They all pasted their finds onto a piece of poster board. When they finished, Sheila took it home with her. She had taken the time to handwrite a poem to go with the board. On the drive back to the house, she had been so occupied with surprising Dirk that she ran a stop sign and a cop pulled her over. The officer wrote her a ticket. She still hadn't told Dirk. It didn't matter anymore. The poster board and the poem had gone out with the garbage on Monday night. Their marriage seemed eager to follow them out.

The therapist's voice jarred Sheila's thoughts. "Well, Dirk," she said, "is what Sheila's saying true? Do you no longer find her desirable?" Her clipped, clinical tone made Sheila's stomach turn sideways again. Not feeling desirable was one thing—having her feelings validated was another. Did the therapist not understand how uncomfortable she was? Sheila's armpits were sweaty. She wanted to excuse herself to go to the restroom. At the same time, she knew she would run out on the session if given the chance. Instead, she pulled a few tissues free of the box on the table and stuffed them under her arms. Let Dirk or the therapist say something to her.

Dirk shook his head and swore. "There's more to it than that." He reached up and played with the hairs at the nape of his neck. His fingers fumbled for length that had been there only months before. He had gotten it cut the same day they cleared him to fly again. Tiny hairs had clung to her lips after she'd kissed his neck that evening. She'd wanted to celebrate his first day back, so she'd wrapped her arms around him and buried her face in his collar. More hair had tickled her nose.

He hadn't been able to stop yawning. He'd wanted to go to sleep so he could be well rested for work the following morning. She did not sleep much at all that night, instead wondering how she could change her looks for him. He did not want her because she was too prim, too proper. She wasn't as raw and passionate as she'd been on the island. She wasn't as exciting. He preferred her as a savage. *There's more to it than that.*

"What more?" Sheila asked. Some part of him still found her attractive. On the island, at least, he had found her attractive. Maybe he had been desperate. There, they were alone. But she remembered the rush of euphoria she'd felt when he brought her the broken bottle filled with water. *I found a stream*, he'd said. *I don't know for sure, but I think it's safe to drink from.* The cold water had stung as it poured over the raw patches in her throat. Hours later, she'd rested against her husband's chest as they laid naked on the sand. It had been the first time they'd had sex since Sheila's miscarriage. She had been so thirsty, and he had filled her up.

Now, Dirk stood and poured himself a glass of water. The liquid spilled from the pitcher into the clear container without effort. Had it been that easy for him to sleep with Cassandra? She wondered how it had happened, how he had met her, how they had carried on a courtship without Sheila knowing. How could she have been so oblivious?

"Dirk," the therapist said, "we're waiting for your answer." She rolled her sleeves up to her elbows. The room was warm— warmer, somehow, than when they had arrived in the office. Sheila thought she had been the only one to notice. A thin line of sweat dotted the therapist's upper lip like a glistening mustache. Sheila, at one point in her adult life, might have laughed. After the island, though, nothing was funny.

"You asked me to kill you," he said. "Every day, every night. At least once an hour." He raised the glass to his mouth but didn't drink. His Adam's apple bobbed. "Don't you understand what that does to a man? You asked me to kill you so many times. I had to think of how to do it. I came up with so many ways—God, it's *disgusting* how creative I was. You cannot imagine what it's like, having your wife beg you to put her out of her misery. You don't know how it feels to hate yourself—it's *my* fault we ended up on that island. You know it as well as I do, even if you've never said it." He took a drink. "I shouldn't have flown after drinking so much."

"I shouldn't have let you."

"You saved our lives. You signaled the boat. Don't you understand? I owe it to you—"

"No," Sheila said, "you don't owe me a thing. I asked you to kill me."

"I was going to kill you. It might have been better."

Sheila could not breathe past the weight on her chest. Moments after the plane went down, a piece of debris had pinned her to the sand. Dirk's voice had pulled her from unconsciousness. When he'd stooped over her, she froze. When she'd smelled the alcohol on his breath, she'd turned her head and vomited. She'd wanted to yell at him, scream at him, punch him in the face. But then he had helped her from the wreckage, and she hadn't had the strength.

The therapist rose. "Are you making threats?"

"No," Dirk said, "I'm saying—"

"There's no need to talk about killing people, then." Her lips formed a line. "Do I make myself clear?"

Dirk nodded.

"Excellent." She sat, turned to a new page in her pad, and started writing. "Whatever feelings you two have for each other now, there's no denying the bond the island created. And in spite of how angry you both are, I'm confident we'll work through these issues and preserve your marriage. Does that sound all right?"

Dirk hesitated. "I want Sheila to be safe. That's all I care about. If you think we can make the marriage work, then I'm ready for it."

"Sheila," the therapist said, "are you on board with that?"

Sheila thought. For the longest time, she had fixated on a happy marriage. In the beginning, everything seemed so hopeful for them. They had a baby on the way, and they cared for each other. But then came the drinking and the baby and the island. She'd asked him to kill her, and he had not done it. But he also had not been the one to save them. In spite of wanting to protect her, he had not been able to rescue her there. She rescued herself.

She rescued herself, and she would rescue this baby. She did not need be with Dirk when she deserved so much better. She did not need to be with anyone. She was more than enough.

Sheila pushed off the couch and stood, looking Dirk in the eye. She clenched her hands into fists, tightened her mouth, and shook her head. "No."

"I beg your pardon?" Dirk asked.

"You don't get to atone," Sheila answered. "You don't get the final say. You want to fix things? You had your chance. I gave you so many chances." She shook her head. "I pitied you in the beginning. Trapped in a marriage with a woman you never loved because she was carrying your child. I thought the drinking made you happier. It made you more accepting. It made you want to be a good father."

He stood and took a step toward her. "You never said any—"

"I'm saying it now." She looked at the therapist, who nodded encouragement. She, like Sheila, must have felt the possibility stretched out between the couple. Maybe she could taste it. Had she ever tasted blood?

"Wait," Dirk said. "We can figure this out."

"I want a divorce," Sheila said.

For the first time in their marriage, Dirk did not speak. He took a step backward and gripped the edge of the bookcase. His eyes widened. He trembled.

"Dirk," the therapist said, "how are you feeling?"

Sheila left before he answered. As she walked out, the therapist tried to stop her. "Bill me later," Sheila said.

The therapist returned to Dirk.

Sheila made a follow-up appointment with the receptionist. Next time, she would be coming alone.

By the time she got downstairs, a taxi waited at the curb. The driver asked her where she wanted to go. She did not know, so she told him her address. He put the car in gear and sipped from a straw shoved into a Big Gulp. Condensation rolled off the plastic. Sheila had not had enough to drink. Somehow, though, she wasn't thirsty.

She flattened a hand against her stomach and watched the streets whiz by the window.

Maybe she would never be thirsty again.

THE MISTAKE HOUSE

THE HOUSE WAS ALL WRONG.

On the outside, it looked fine—blue Victorian two-story, gray shingles, the brown door that Mom despised. One porch swing with a chain that could snap at any moment. A minuscule yard with grass just short of dying, a paved walkway to the street.

Inside, the layout changed. Rooms switched places every day. Hallways tipped toward hell; they listed left and tripped their occupants. Floors inclined or declined without explanation, without consistency. Lights flickered, but that was the least shocking thing that happened in the house.

We moved in seven months ago, and we should have moved out right away. The house was all wrong then, and now, so are we.

On our last day, I awoke in the middle of the night. My bed had moved across the room. I sat up and hit my head against the window sill, which was then halfway up the wall.

I rubbed my skull and stared at my door, much farther away than it had been. That was nothing new.

But my mother's scream was.

Throwing off the covers, I leaped out of bed and ran toward the door. The floor lurched beneath me. My stomach lurched with it. Wood and metal groaned as the room changed shape again. I froze. I didn't have time for this.

"Laurie!"

My mother's voice struck my spine like an arrow. Goosebumps rose on my arms. "I'm on my way!"

She screamed again, but this time, her voice didn't form any words. The floor stopped moving. I didn't waste any time examining the new layout. Instead, I burst through my doorway and staggered out into the hall—and promptly froze again.

Normally, Mom's room sat next to mine. Now it glowed at the end of the hall—a beacon in the darkness, thanks to the lamp on her nightstand. I sprinted toward it without thinking and hurtled into the room without stopping to reorient myself.

What I saw there stopped my heart.

The furniture in my mom's room had become a tangled mess. Her desk and bookcase formed a misshapen totem pole, with books sticking out of the wood in all directions. Her bed, split in half, cornered the desk/bookcase mutant like bookends. An enormous chasm spanned the floor. Instead of revealing the living room below, it opened into an insane abyss.

But that was all tame stuff, compared to my mother.

The abomination—as that was all I could think of when I looked at what had been my mother—stood impossibly tall and thin, like it had been stretched out almost to breaking. It waved its useless, flesh-colored tentacles at me and flashed jagged teeth from the mouth in its chest. Its eyes were massive—one winked from its hip, the other leaked tears at the creature's stomach.

I could only watch, helpless, as I felt my bones break and my organs switch places.

The house wasn't only rearranging its interior.

It was rearranging us.

THE JOB

LUTHER HOLBROOK HAD BEEN KILLING PEOPLE FOR THE PAST seven years.

"You're a goddamn natural," Katie Kingsley, his partner, said. But after being in the business for ten years, she would know. She was the one who got Luther into fulfilling hits after they both came home from the war. Katie was a short woman with dark hair, dark eyes, and rows of golden teeth. Someone had knocked out the original set in combat. Teeth that glinted in the sun were a hazard in their line of work. She opened her mouth as little as possible.

At ten o'clock at night on Christmas Eve, Luther and Katie were out on a rush job. Before each assassination the two of them carried out, they received a stack of papers regarding their target. Their boss, Riddick, sealed these papers in a manila envelope marked *Confidential*. The file contained the target's background, criminal record, and photographic identification.

Katie and Luther were supposed to review the contents of the envelope together. This time, they hadn't. It was Christmas, and they wanted to enjoy it, and as much as they both hated these last-minute gigs, completion paid double. Money always won out.

Outside, the frigid air burned Luther's nose and throat. He and Katie trudged through the forest in search of their target. Skeleton trees cast eerie shadows on the path. Branches cracked beneath the weight of ice and snow. Otherwise, the woods were silent.

Silent night, holy night.

Luther shivered as he hummed the song. He was supposed to attend candlelight Mass with his sister and her husband. They felt sorry for him because he lived alone. They had no idea what he did for a living. Luther's target wouldn't get to go to Mass.

"We've been walking around for ages," Luther said.

"I know," Katie replied. "Not much farther, I promise."

"I don't see any red roofs, Katie. Could we maybe have passed it?"

She smacked him on the back of the head.

The only sounds for a long time were cracking trees and crunching boots.

All is calm, all is bright.

Luther hadn't been to Mass since the previous Christmas Eve. He'd gone to confession, as he did every candlelight Mass.

Bless me, Father, for I have sinned. It's been a year since my last confession.

Father Evans's disgust struck Luther through the screen of separation. *May God give you pardon and peace.*

He couldn't have meant it.

I absolve you from your sins.

"There." Katie nodded toward a house with a red roof and a smoking chimney.

"You're sure?" Luther asked.

She kicked his leg. "Come on."

———

THEIR TARGET WAS SHOWERING WHEN THEY BROKE IN. WHEN Luther's hammer broke the window, the sound of running water from down the hallway filled the air. Without wanting or meaning to, Luther thought about christening. No one had christened him as a baby.

This holy water shall wash away thy sins and the mark of thy iniquity.

Round yon virgin Mother and child.

"What are we going to do?" Luther asked.

"We could break the door down."

"Hell no, we can't. I'm not seeing him naked."

Katie scowled. "You have the same parts."

"I know that," he said, "but I don't want to see his."

"You were in the *military*. How in holy hell . . . ?"

The window they chose opened into the living room. There was a tan microfiber couch with two red pillows, a glass coffee table, and a massive bookcase. No television. A miniature Nativity scene sat on the top of the table. There was straw spread inside and around it to simulate the floor of a barn. The wise men gathered at the edge of the Nativity scene, almost out of sight. A donkey, sheep, rooster, and cow huddled together on the opposite side of the scene. Mary and Joseph stood behind the manger. Baby Jesus was absent.

Holy infant so tender and mild.

"Jesus is missing," Luther said.

"Mary's there. You're Catholic, isn't that enough?"

"I guess so." Luther sat on the couch and propped his feet on the table.

Katie sat beside him. "We can't mess this one up. Headshot."

"Does he deserve it?"

"Luther."

"I'm listening."

"You execute. I'll clean up." Katie shrugged off her coat. A layer of snow settled against the couch.

"Hell of a job with that so far," Luther said.

Katie reached into the pocket of the coat and withdrew a bottle of bleach and two pairs of rubber gloves. She handed a pair of gloves to Luther.

"I'm already wearing gloves."

"Do you want to get blood on them? God, you are stupid."

Luther took the pistol out of the holster at his hip. He'd asked for a revolver, but he hadn't gotten one. The boss wanted him to shoot the target at close range. It would look more like suicide that way.

"I need to write the note," Katie said. "Do you know the guy's name?"

"No, I thought you did."

"Didn't you read the file?"

"No," Luther said, "and neither did you."

"Damn it." Katie got up from the couch and went over to the bookcase. She pulled a thick volume off the shelf and flipped it open. Her fingers ripped a page loose.

"What the hell are you doing?"

"Paper. We'll make do."

Luther thought about what he'd be saying at confession. He was supposed to tell the priest every dirty deed since last Christmas Eve. At confession, a person started with mortal sin and moved on to venial sin afterward. Luther never made it past mortal sins.

Tell me your sins so I may absolve you.

I've murdered twenty-two people since my last confession. I killed them for money.

How do you feel?

Terrible, Father. My soul is so heavy.

Katie waved the finished note in Luther's face. She'd written the words in cherry-red lipstick that clashed against the stark black print.

"Lipstick?" Luther asked. "Why the hell did you use lipstick? Are there women here?"

"It's mine, moron. I forgot to bring a pen."

"Holy hell, we're going to get it."

The water in the shower stopped. Luther and Katie looked at each other. "You're up," Katie said.

"At least let him get dressed first."

Katie rolled her eyes. "What if he hears us talking?"

"Just shut your damn mouth."

I absolve you of your sins.

I absolve you.

Pray the rosary.

Oh, Father. My Father. It won't be enough.

Katie pinched Luther's arm until he snapped out of his trance.

"What the hell?" he asked.

"You just spaced out. We have a job to do."

Luther chambered a bullet and held the gun in his left hand. He had to get it together. He was going to see this job completed. He could worry about his soul once his work was finished.

Footsteps sounded on the carpet from the room at the end of the hall. The doorknob clicked.

He's coming, Katie mouthed.

Luther leveled the pistol. He didn't expect to see Father Evans emerge from his bedroom.

Father Evans, to his credit, also didn't expect to see Luther.

"Luther." Father Evans froze. "What are you doing he—is that a gun?"

"You know him?" Katie asked.

The pistol shook in Luther's hand. His grip and aim were much less certain. If he'd read the file like he was supposed to, he would've seen Father Evans's picture. He would've recognized the blue-eyed, bald man with the turned-up nose. He could've passed the case to someone less involved.

"Please." Father Evans put his hands up in the air. He was wearing his collar and robes already, although midnight Mass wasn't for several hours.

"Father," Luther said.

Katie said, "Shoot him."

A drop of sweat slid down the side of Father Evans's face. It could've been a tear.

Luther remembered how he'd gone to confession for the first time on the job so many years ago. He'd stumbled into the booth to escape his sister's prying eyes. Once he was inside, the partition had opened. He'd seen the same blue eyes he stared into now.

Bless me, Father, for I have sinned. Absolve me of my guilt.

Luther couldn't be absolved.

"Hail, Mary, full of grace. The Lord thy God is with thee." Father Evans dropped to his knees on the floor and bowed his head. "Blessed art thou amongst women and blessed is the fruit of thy womb, Jesus."

Father Evans clutched a rosary. Luther's stomach tied itself in a complicated knot. The gun tumbled from his fingers and clattered on the table.

"Get it together." Katie reached for the pistol.

Luther knocked it to the ground.

Katie whirled around and punched Luther. Luther toppled

backward, clutching his nose as she picked up the gun, aimed it at Father Evans, and pulled the trigger. The gun discharged with a hollow thud, courtesy of the silencer.

Blood spilled onto the couch and splattered on the wall. The bullet went in, but it never came out. Katie was a good shot.

A trickle of blood dripped from the hole in Father Evans's forehead. He stayed upright for a few seconds before slumping sideways against the wall. His eyes, Luther noticed, were still wet with tears.

Sleep in heavenly peace.

Katie walked over to the body and put the pistol in Father Evans's hand. She picked up the bottle of bleach and went back to the couch.

Blood dripped out of Luther's nose. His hands were sticky with it. The dark red liquid oozed onto his lap and coated part of the couch.

"I need you to move," Katie said.

"Too bad. Go to hell."

Katie set the bleach down and slipped into her coat. "I don't have time for this. Riddick wanted us finished by five. You can walk back to the compound."

Luther said nothing as Katie set a baseball down on the ground in front of the window. She shimmied through the broken pane of glass and disappeared without a backward glance.

Luther got up from the couch. He picked up the bloody cushion and dragged it behind him as he walked over to Father Evans's body. The wound in his forehead didn't bleed much. The bullet plugged the hole. The eyes were still open. Luther's skin crawled.

Turning his head, Luther set the cushion on the floor behind the body. He slipped his arm around Father Evans's shoulders and slid him down until he rested on the cushion. Now the blood looked natural. Luther wrapped the rosary around the priest's hand, reached over, and closed the unseeing blue eyes.

Sleep in heavenly peace.

ACKNOWLEDGMENTS

I have *so many people* to thank for helping me bring this book to life. My partner, Gabe, for supporting me and believing in me no matter what. My friend, Sam, to whom this collection is dedicated, for appreciating my writing and tolerating my weirdness.

Thank you to Kealan Patrick Burke and Elderlemon Design for giving me such a beautiful cover. Thank you to Scott Moses and Todd Keisling for your invaluable insights and feedback. Thanks also to my editor, proofreader, and friend Rae Oestreich. I'm so lucky to know you, all of you.

To my Kickstarter backers . . . this book wouldn't be published without you. That's not hyperbole—I didn't have the funds on my own. Specifically, thanks to the following people:

- Guest 1778900365
- Aidan, Kristin Anderson-Terpstra
- Angelicide
- John Anuci
- Brian Asman
- AvalonRoselin

- The Creative Fund by BackerKit
- Brian Baer
- Patrick Barb
- Deshana Barua
- Ryan Beal
- Christopher Beard
- Gwendolen Benjamin
- Adam Bertolett
- Sonora Bostian
- Rachel Brantley
- Brian, Brittany
- Andrew Brown
- Luke Rudmann Browning
- Tom Butler
- Angela Bybee
- George C
- John C
- Mariah Caban
- Kara Cargill
- Michelle Carl
- Allie Carney
- Mel Cartaya
- Lexie Carver
- Cathy
- Anastasia Catris
- Cecilysleven
- ChildishRevolt88
- Paul Childs
- Ckrovatin
- Dennis Clarke
- Ray Clydesdale
- Andrew Cook
- Chris Cooper
- Matt Corley

- Nick Cort
- Coryl
- Joe Costa
- L.E. D.
- Cassie Lola Daley
- Dana
- Jeremy S Daugherty
- Dustin Davis
- David DiCarlo
- Shawna Duckworth
- Stig Dyrdal
- Anthony E
- Samantha E.
- Em
- Esa Eriksson
- Emma Fink
- Ash Flanagan
- Becca Futrell
- GD
- Alberto Gonzalez
- Matt Graupman
- Elysa Gray-Saito
- Diana Griffin
- Hallowqueen
- Samantha Harner
- Sadie Hartmann
- Richard Hausen
- Heather
- Richard Hebson
- Emily Herrington
- Michael Hirtzy
- Becky Holland
- Eric Holt
- Joshua Hurd

- CW Younts III
- Max Booth III
- Katie Irving
- John J. Walsh IV
- Clare J
- Jake
- Michael Janes
- Janelle Janson
- Jax
- Aaron Jeffries
- Jenna
- Norma JMB
- Juliana Johnson
- Jordan
- Kirsten Jorgensen
- William Gustkey Jr
- Karen Kaderli
- Cassie Kelley
- Shaun Kenyon
- The Splendiferous Laboratory
- Dre Lasana
- Zach Lay
- Alexis Lebow-Wolf
- Brianna Leclerc
- Kevin Lemke
- Leslie
- Justin Lewis
- John Lynch
- Dave Machado
- Maddy
- Marleigh
- Jasmin Marquez
- Jes Martindale
- Christopher Dean McAfee

- Michael McCaffrey
- Ashley McGrath
- Shawn McVicker
- Victor Meng
- merinda
- Caitlin Michielsen
- Dakota Miller
- Mirintala
- Bryan F. Moose
- Aaron Moxcey
- Kristen Muenz
- NaddyF
- Martin Nicchetta
- Irwing Nieto
- Noah
- Chan Chung On
- Oscar Ornelas
- Richard Parker
- Chris Parsons
- Kevin Patterson
- Alex Pearson
- Tim Pedersen
- joe pesavento
- Marcy Plasencia
- Kent Lee Platte
- Liz Powalisz
- Michael Powell
- T R
- Rachel
- Emily Reed
- Krystine "Reese"
- Katie Reitzel
- Ruby Ricaldi
- William Robertson

- Tracy Robinson
- Jen S
- Anita gray Saito
- Nikki Sanchez
- Scorthosaurus
- Scott
- Kim Segers
- John Shalom
- Joseph Sherer
- Juliette Sicard
- silentknight
- Kenneth Skaldebø
- Benjamin Smith
- Eric Smith
- Charlie Stark
- Angela Steiner
- Stewie
- Michael S Sturgis
- Kieron Tan
- Savannah Tanbusch
- Alex Tangkilisan
- Andrew Tate
- Jordan Taylor
- Shrader Thomas
- Heather Tieck
- Tom
- Ronald Tremblay
- Trinity Turner
- David Umland
- Ashley Uveges
- Derrick Vann
- Jason Varner
- w0lfsbane
- Colin Walsh

- Jax Wells
- Karmen Wells
- Mark Wheaton
- WhoIsTheGreatCarlozo
- Angel Williams
- DJ Wilson
- Matthew Wilson
- Kimberly Wix
- Rebecca May Womack
- Devon Woods
- Zandaia

Thank you all so, so much for your support and encouragement along the way. It means more to me than you can imagine. Because of you, I get to keep doing what I love. There is no better feeling in the world.

ABOUT THE AUTHOR

Briana Morgan is a horror author and playwright. Her books include *The Tricker-Treater and Other Stories, Unboxed, Livingston Girls, A Writer's Guide to Slaying Social, Reflections, Touch: A One-Act Play*, and *Blood and Water*. She is also a proud member of the Horror Writers Association.

When she's not writing, Briana enjoys watching horror movies, playing video games, cosplaying, and spending time with her partner and cats. Other interests include falling down YouTube rabbit holes, exploring spooky places, and snacking.

Printed in Great Britain
by Amazon

52507565R00061